Shadows of Exile

RETURN OF
THE AFRICAN KING

MOMAR NJAI

ISBN: 978-0-578-54076-4

Printed in the United States

To those within the shadows…

Prologue

RETURN OF THE AFRICAN KING

Ancient Malian Empire, Late 1280s to 1337

According to ancient history, King Mansa Musa I was the richest king that ever walked the earth. He had an estimated net worth of $400 billion, which dwarfs the likes of John D. Rockefeller, Carlos Slim, Bill Gates, Warren Buffet, and even Jeff Bezos by current standards. The kingship of Mansa Musa was revered throughout the African continent and the entire world. In his youth, Musa grew under the tutelage of his great-uncle, King Abu Bakr II, learning the king's ways and becoming devoted to the love and worship of Allah.

King Abu Bakr II was highly regarded throughout Africa, but even in all his glory, he still felt incomplete. Night after night, he stayed awake, staring at his throne, thinking about the many responsibilities he bore and wondering whether he would ever have the chance to fulfill his greatest desire in life.

Though he had a great love for his people, he had a desire that was even greater than this love—he wanted to tour the world and see the ends of the Atlantic Ocean. Abu Bakr had been fascinated by the oceans since he was a child. On many days, he stood by the shore and wondered where all the waters originated from and how far the oceans stretched. Even the throne, in all its majesty and opulence, could not take this obsession away from him. Determined to embark on a journey to lay his curiosity to rest, Abu Bakr wondered who he could trust to oversee his throne while he was gone.

One day, Abu Bakr announced to his council, "I shall be going on a journey around the world. I will be away for a long time, and I have found someone to replace me while I'm gone. I assure you he is the best person to wear the crown of this great empire."

He waved at one of his royal guards, who walked into the hallway while the councilmen held their breath in suspense, wondering who their king had chosen to stand in his place.

Three royal guards and two maidens bearing vessels of gold entered from the hallway, parting to reveal Abu Bakr's choice—a young man named Musa Keita. He stood over six feet tall, was well built, and had around him an intimidating aura of grace. His skin was olive black and the hair on his head was the color of midnight, glistening ever so slightly in the sun. His broad shoulders, which seemed to grow wider as he drew closer to the council chamber, made obvious the great confidence he had in himself.

"I present to you my grand-nephew, Musa Keita. He shall be your interim king while I'm away. I have taught him all of my ways, and I have seen him speak with much wisdom and shown our people love. There are no better hands I can trust to hold this mantle and keep these beautiful smiles on the faces of our people."

Musa Keita bowed before King Abu Bakr, and then he turned to the councilmen. They all stood and bowed to pledge their allegiance to their new king.

Over the next days, thousands of soldiers loaded hundreds of boats and ships with food, water, gold, and other supplies; enough to sustain them and the king for many months. The people of Mali gathered at the shore to bid King Abu Bakr farewell as he embarked on this journey, which he had long desired.

"Musa, these are your people. Treat them with fairness and don't do anything that would bring shame to the kingdom," Abu Bakr whispered to Musa as he handed over the golden mantle and the crown. Musa nodded and promised Abu Bakr he would be a great ruler.

"My wisdom is with you, Son," Abu Bakr said as he waved at the crowd. He then pulled up his loose-fitting boubou and boarded his ship. Thousands of soldiers boarded the other vessels, and they set sail while the newly crowned king and others waved until they lost sight of the boats in the glare of the rising sun, which cast bright rays of light on the blue sea.

For many months, Musa Keita ruled the empire of Mali without incident. Many days and nights, he walked to the shores and cast his eyes to the far end of the waters, hoping to catch a glimpse of his uncle's vessel. He prayed for Allah to be with the king, to guide him in his search for fulfillment, and to bring him back safely to return to his throne.

Beneath all the glamour and majestic opulence of the kingdom, the load of leadership weighed heavily on Musa. There were many legal cases to preside over and endless decisions to make. Decisions that would determine the life and destiny of hundreds of thousands of people. Every day, as Musa walked up to the throne to sit with the council of elders, he felt his heart beating hard against his chest. *Will I be able to make decisions as wise as my uncle would have made? Would he be happy with this?* he often wondered. He routinely prayed to Allah for wisdom to rule justly and the ability to provide happiness to his people without letting his personal emotions get in the way.

One day, Musa heard an unusual amount of noise coming from the king's court. He hurried in and saw royal guards standing beside a man accused of a crime and a great multitude cheering as they leveled allegations against the man. The judges were seated, waiting to pass their verdict on the man, when Musa Keita entered. As soon as they saw him, everyone in the court stood and bowed in reverence. Musa Keita looked at the young man standing behind the dock crying. He had been beaten so badly that his mouth was swollen, and his cheeks bled.

"What's his crime?" Musa asked.

"He is an infidel," a judge announced. "On several occasions, he was found praying to a god other than Allah, right inside a house east of the central mosque, while *Jummah* prayer was happening."

In those days, Islam was the only religion practiced in Mali. Anyone seen praying to a god other than Allah, including wooden statues, was considered an infidel, an enemy of the state, who had to be cast away. According to the law of Islam, all Muslims faced east—the direction of the *Qibla*, which points toward the holy city of Mecca—whenever they prayed. There was no death penalty stated for infidels in ancient Mali, however it was a great abomination for that man to disobey the laws of Islam by praying to another god at the same time Muslims were observing *Jummah* prayers. It was believed that his infidelity would stand as a stumbling block, preventing their prayers from getting to Allah.

"If *Jummah* prayers were ongoing at the central mosque, then how did anyone see him? Would they not have been offering prayers to the almighty Allah?" the young king asked thoughtfully.

That question bewildered the judges and caused them to become mute until the same judge who accused the man spoke again. This time, his voice was lower and an expression of shame clouded his face. He admitted that they had planted someone to watch the man after rumors had spread that he was an infidel.

"Let him go!" Musa commanded, to the surprise of everyone. "Who are you to judge, in the place of Allah, those who decide to go another path? Allah is all-supreme and all-powerful to fight his own battles and recall his lost sheep."

As he spoke, Musa walked to the front porch and stood beside the chief judge, where everyone could see him clearly.

"The goal of Islam is to spread the peaceful message of Allah through his holy prophet all over the world. For the non-believers, may Allah touch their hearts, open their eyes, and make them see the light. By attempting to hang them and spill blood, you're trying to take the place of God."

A grave silence fell on the crowd. The judges cast their faces to the ground, and a little smile crept onto the face of the accused man.

"Even as Muslims, we must learn not to think less of the man who does not sprout a beard or the woman who does not wear a hijab," Musa continued. "Their struggle is different from your struggle; their ways are different from your ways. You may have perfected your innermost man, and they too may have done the same without you knowing.

"Let not this mirage of righteousness you put on to deceive others come back to deceive you, because, on that day of reckoning, that beardless brother or that sister who you condemned for not wearing a hijab may walk into Jinnah, leaving you in the queue of people waiting for Allah's wrath."

A cloak of silence enveloped the courtroom and remained long after Musa walked away. He demanded that the royal guards bring him all their records so he might read through to know if the judges had been fair in their verdicts.

* * *

Many more months passed without any word of King Abu Bakr. Then, one day, a single boat anchored at the shore. After receiving word, Musa Keita hurried to the boat, which was already surrounded by the inquisitive eyes of those eager to see if their king had returned. The soldiers in the ship were distraught, however, and wouldn't speak until they saw Musa Keita. The interim king soon approach them in a flowing white caftan, elated to finally hand the reins of power back to his great-uncle.

Musa eyes grew wide in shock when he saw the soldiers but no sign of his uncle. "Where is the captain?" he asked, his voice shaky and his face colored with agony.

The captain climbed out of the boat and fell at Musa's feet.

"Captain, where is the king?" Musa repeated.

"Oh, my prince!" the captain cried. "We navigated for a long period until we saw in the midst of the ocean a great whirlpool with a massive current. All of the boats, including that of your great-uncle, our king, have been destroyed, and those on board have perished. My boat was the last one. When I realized what was happening, I turned sail and was able to escape the current."

Musa did not believe him. He could not believe that his uncle—a man who had been so fascinated with water all his life, could so easily perish at sea. A man who despite his royal heritage, chose to be a captain and had sailed hundreds of ships until the reigns of leadership fell on him after his own father died. If any man knew how to navigate through a whirlpool, even in the face of a bloody storm, it would be his uncle. "This doesn't make sense!" he barked.

Musa Keita sent thousands of soldiers to go search for his great-uncle, Abu Bakr, but after several weeks of futile search, Musa, and everyone else in the empire, came to accept that their king would never return. Musa and the whole community mourned the loss of their great king according to the laws of Islam.

Following the death of the Abu Bakr, Musa Keita was crowned *Mansa*, the highest title in the Malian empire, meaning "emperor" or "mighty king" in the Mandinka language. He was now Mansa Musa I. And though he had been serving in the role of king since his uncle had departed, Mansa Musa now looked upon the Malian Empire with the eyes of a king for the first time. It dawned on him that his role as a king had at last truly begun and it was his job to make his empire the greatest in Africa and in the entire world.

Having gone through the verdicts of the previous months and years, Mansa Musa let go of most of the old judges and replaced them with new ones. He freed the prisoners who were sentenced unjustly and stopped the unfair treatment of the minority clans. He built houses for the poor, schools for children, libraries, hospitals, and a university in Timbuktu, the biggest in Africa in those ancient times.

During his reign, Mali was blessed with discoveries of huge deposits of gold and salt. No other empire in the world had as much gold as what flowed from within Mali's borders. All of that gold, as was tradition in the empire, belonged to the king, and with it, he made the lives of his people beautiful. Mansa Musa was generous with his wealth. Word spread from the north to the west, east, and south, and kings from all over the world heard about Mansa Musa's might and came in droves to pay allegiance to him, to make friends, and to seek help in times of need.

With his wealth waxing stronger by the day, Mansa Musa's army increased in strength. His soldiers won many battles, reclaimed lost parts of the empire, and made their enemies surrender. Mansa Musa built trade centers all over the empire, with people coming from across the Atlantic and the Middle East to trade in gold and salt.

After he had set up Mali to be the envy of other neighboring empires, Mansa Musa decided it was finally time for him to perform the greatest ritual he needed to perform as a devout Muslim: a visit to the holy city of Mecca (hajj). For many years, Mansa Musa planned his hajj. He wanted to be the greatest Muslim to walk the earth, and he knew that this hajj would be his opportunity to spread Islam all over the world.

At sunrise on the day of his departure, sixty thousand men stood at the city gate waiting for the king to make his grand appearance. Each one bore hundreds of gold bars packed in handheld bags. Beside them were heralds dressed in silk clothing and holding gold staffs, standing beside camels and horses on whose backs were bags of gold dust.

Mansa Musa arrived at the city gate with the councilmen and his son, Maghan Musa, who looked very much like him. Maghan knelt down, and Mansa Musa gave him the golden staff of leadership.

"Keep the land in my wisdom and benevolence," he said to his son as he presented him to the people as the king who would rule over them while he was away.

Mansa Musa bid his family and councilmen goodbye, straddled his horse, and rode off in the company of sixty thousand men. As Mansa Musa and his men journeyed from one empire to the next on their way to Mecca, masses of people came out to see them. Many of them had heard

Shadows of Exile

of his might and his riches, and they wanted to see it for themselves. Others heard the sounds of the hooves of the thousands of horses and camels approaching their lands, and they ran away, scared that the great king had come with his soldiers to wipe them out and take over their lands. When they saw that it was just a man peacefully going on his way with his convoy to worship his God, the frightened inhabitants, who had hidden among the city walls, the rocks, and the forests, began to file out. They cheered and waved at Mansa Musa, and he gave some of them enough gold to make them wealthy for a lifetime.

From Medina to Cairo, Mansa Musa gave out gold bars and gold dust to the poor and even to kings who hosted him and his men. Sixty thousand men were more than enough to do any job he wanted, so Mansa Musa built mosques every Friday in whatever country or city he found himself. At that time, the whole world was in awe of his wealth. People came from far and near to journey with him because they knew their lives would be changed forever.

Because many poor people in Cairo, Medina, and the other cities in the Mediterranean through which King Mansa Musa had passed had received portions of gold, a great inflation befell the territory. The price of food skyrocketed, and the price of gold fell significantly. Before Mansa Musa arrived in Mecca, he heard of the inflation. This was not what he had planned; he had only wanted to share his wealth. Thus, he considered how he might make this right. On his way back from Mecca, he borrowed all of the gold he could from moneylenders in Medina and Cairo and promised to pay them back at high interest. He took it back to Mali. Once again, gold became scarce, and its value gradually began to rise again. This was the first and only time one man controlled the value of gold across the entire Mediterranean.

Mansa Musa returned from Mecca with more than the gold. He also brought with him many architects and Islamic scholars. They were so prolific in their work that, at the peak of Mansa Musa's reign, he had built over four hundred cities. Years after the death of Mansa Musa, the amount of gold mined from the Malian empire depreciated, but there was still enough wealth to last the empire for hundreds of generations. From generation to generation, Mansa Musa's throne, glory, and wealth passed down through his bloodline, finally reaching the hands of King Idris, a king who swore to do even more for the kingdom than what Mansa Musa I did, and preserve the great family legacy.

Chapter One

"Allahu Akbar!"

"Allahu Akbar!"

King Idris and his two teenage sons, Musa and Hamza, bowed again as the voice of the imam rang out from the central mosque, creating a seraphic atmosphere on that cool evening. From his mat, which was laid in front of the mats of his sons, the king led the boys in offering their prayers to the almighty Allah. When they were done praying, the boys bowed slightly to their father and headed down the stairs, with three servants bearing the prayer mats behind them. Hamza was named after one of the king's trusted allies, while Musa bore the name of his great ancestor Mansa Musa I.

Standing on the top porch of his palace, King Idris rested his arms on the golden railings and looked out into the city center, watching his people as they filed out of the central mosque. It was a market day in Sikasso. There were women bearing baskets of yams and tomatoes; babies strapped to their mothers' backs by pieces of fabric wrapped around them and tied across their mothers' chests; and men carrying many gallons of palm wine.

It had been a year of bountiful harvest, and King Idris was happy that his people were making profits from their farm produce. Still, he couldn't help but imagine what their lives would be like when the project he was working on was complete.

"These city walls," he said to himself, "will not contain the riches that will flow in this land because everyone will be swimming in an ocean of wealth."

King Idris waved his hand, and his butler, Alika, a dark, heavyset, gray-bearded man, came closer with a tray holding a cup of juice. He gave the king the cup, bowed slowly, and receded to a spot a few steps behind the monarch. King Idris took a sip of his juice and allowed his imagination to run wild. All he had ever wanted was to give his people the perfect life, not only to provide them with everything they needed to be comfortable, but also to empower them to create wealth. He wished for every family in Mali to be wealthy, for not even a single family to ever be called poor again. King Idris envisioned a land where poverty was only a myth, a land where there were no beggars on the streets, where every man could afford to give his family a good life. He wanted to build a model country that the rest of the world would talk about forever. This was the grand aim he set for himself, and he spent his days and nights thinking about how to make it happen.

From his great ancestor King Mansa Musa I to his father, Idris's predecessors had made the people their priority, using the proceeds from Mali's vast deposits of gold to feed the people and make their lives flourish. For centuries, they had traded in gold and other natural resources. The royal family had accumulated and preserved so much wealth that now, long after Mali's known gold deposits had been excavated, the royal coffers were still full enough to sustain the empire for hundreds of generations.

Still, King Idris wanted more. He didn't just want to be the king who provided for his people; he wanted to be the king who empowered all African nations to take control of their destiny. He wanted to restore the vast continent to its glory days when poverty, war, famine, and disease didn't exist. He wanted to take the empire to such a height that scholars from around the world would come in droves to study their civilization, and Western cities would begin to model themselves after Mali. For the nearly two decades he had been on the throne, Idris had thought about how he could do this, but his dreams had always seemed out of his reach—until eight months ago.

* * *

He had been at this very spot on the upper porch of his hallowed palace when he had received a call from the construction company he had hired to build a new power plant in the *Kéniéba Valley*. The valley was a vast, isolated area that had been abandoned for many years, making it the safest place to build the power plant. It also turned out to be a place of great fortune. While clearing and preparing the site, the construction company had discovered some unknown metals. Further testing revealed them to be gold deposits that stretched for miles in the rock bed beneath the swamplands.

King Idris immediately took the royal convoy to the site to see with his own eyes the wonder that would cause all his dreams to come true. It had been a long time since the last of Mali's gold had been extracted; everyone believed that there were no more deposits. But as the king held up one of the glinting pieces of metal, watching it shimmer in the light of the setting sun, he knew that the days ahead were going to be the best the empire had ever seen.

The king hired miners to scout around the valley for other gold deposits, and in the weeks that followed, ten new deposits, estimated to be worth hundreds of billions of dollars, were found.

* * *

"*Allahu Akbar!*" The king raised his hand slightly and whispered a prayer as he recalled that golden day. "God has given us the power to rise again. Better than we ever have."

He raised his glass toward Alika, who smiled and nodded. The king then gulped down the remainder of his juice and handed the empty cup to the butler. Alika placed it on his tray and retreated to a pillar near where the guards stood.

Just then, two special messengers dressed in golden capes approached the porch, the tail ends of their uniforms sweeping the glistening floor behind them. They knelt before the king and offered adulations. "Live forever, Your Majesty, the king of kings whose glory glitters in the sun and shines brighter than the moon at night."

The king turned and touched their shoulders with the beaded end of his royal cane.

"A letter arrived for you, Your Majesty," one messenger said, presenting a coffee-brown envelope.

The king took the letter, and the messengers stood and left. Fury overtook King Idris when he read the letter. Immediately he sent word to the nation's elders and wise men, summoning them to his palace that same evening.

* * *

The councilmen gathered in the hallowed chamber, exchanging pleasantries and speaking in low tones. They came in caftans and boubous of different colorful shades, each flowing along as they walked. Their heads were wrapped with large turbans that covered all but a small portion of their faces and hung down generously to just above their chests. As the men talked about their daily lives, wives, children, and businesses, they heard the sound of the royal flute announcing the king. Every man quickly went to stand by his seat to await King Idris's arrival. When they saw him gracefully walking down the stairs and approaching the chamber with three of his royal guards behind him, the councilmen all went down on one knee, bowed their heads, and called in unison, "Long live the king."

King Idris took his place on his throne, which was embellished with shining precious stones along its arms and had two colossal elephant tusks that curved toward each other at the top. On his head, King Idris wore a golden crown; his neck was adorned with rows of royal beads, which rested on his generously embroidered, pearl-studded boubou, gracing him with the aura of royalty. With a wave of his hand, the councilmen sat down and the king began to speak.

"I called you all here because this throne is incomplete without you. From the day of my ascension, I swore to consult you in all my decisions because the kingdom belongs to us all. This morning, I received a letter." He waved his hand, and a royal servant brought the paper, gave it to him, bowed, and walked back to his position. "A letter from a Chinese corporation. They're interested in our newly discovered gold deposits, and they're offering us a deal—$300 billion to lease the mines for fifty years."

He paused for a moment and observed the faces of the councilmen. Some looked excited, others were indifferent, and a few seemed slighted by the message.

He couldn't help but notice the way the eyes of his brother—Abdulsalaam Mahmoud, who was standing at the other end of the room—lit up at the mention of $300 billion.

"Tempting offer, we may all agree, but we have to remember that it goes contrary to our plans. When the expatriates came some weeks ago to look at the site, they said it was out of curiosity for what they called 'the unending wealth of resources in Africa.' We did not know they were assessing it to make this offer." He held the paper between the tips of two fingers and waved it a little as he spoke. "Now we have two options before us. We can either take the easier and quicker way and hand over our treasures to foreign powers, like other African nations have done, or be patient, take our time, and invest in mining equipment, building refineries, and whatever else is needed, so we'll be in total control of our wealth and destiny."

The elders were plunged deep into thought. Shortly after the new gold deposits had been discovered, King Idris had decreed that the empire would build its own gold refinery, with every family in the empire of Mali a shareholder. They had already contracted with experts from Asia who were working day and night to complete the refinery in three years. It was King Idris's most significant legacy, a legacy that would make every family in the empire wealthy. The refinery would not only provide jobs for the people, but each family would also have their share, from which they would receive a steady flow of income.

After some whispering among the councilmen, Chief Abonive raised his hand, and the king asked him to speak.

"We are a people of repute," he began. "All over the world, we are known to be blessed with riches. We are not poor people that can be swayed with a pot of porridge. I suggest that we keep our eyes on the bigger picture, the picture of our own making, and reject this offer."

Sounds of affirmation rang throughout the chambers. He had said what many were thinking. Chief Abonive sat, and another councilman, Mallam Tanko, who was a known contrarian, stood. Immediately, hissing sounds came from all corners of the chambers. If it were in their power, most of the councilmen would have banned him from their meetings, for he always had something argumentative to say.

The king also had his reservations about the man, but he kept them hidden. He believed that Mallam Tanko often did the things he did just for the sake of being controversial. If it were not so, why did he vote against the Scholar Program of the king's court, a scheme to sponsor some of the most outstanding students to study medicine and technology at Ivy League schools in America so they could return to Mali and contribute greatly to the economy? If not for the vain desire to be the topic of every conversation, what else could have made Mallam Tanko vote against building a new complex for the state police? Mallam Tanko was a nutcase, and the king was deliberately giving him a long rope.

"This is a time that will test the faith of every one of us," Mallam Tanko began.

"Of course," the king muttered under his breath. It was very typical of Mallam Tanko to begin with grandiose statements and end with rebellion.

"It is time for us to stand our ground," Mallam Tanko continued, much to everyone's surprise. "The discovery of these vast gold deposits is the best thing that has ever happened to us, and anyone who wants to take them from us should be seen as an enemy of the state." He looked around and saw the surprised faces staring at him. "So, I stand with the king. Let's be patient and birth our own legacy."

If they had been at a conference, the councilmen would have given him a loud clap, but because they were in the palace, they instead nodded and hummed in affirmation. Some councilmen suggested that they shouldn't make hasty decisions, instead, they should all go home and think over it. On the other hand, a more significant number of them said that the issue didn't hold water; after all, fifty years was a long time to hand over one's heritage to foreigners. The meeting ended and the councilmen collected their hampers from the royal maids and then dispersed. Abdulsalaam Mahmoud, however, remained at his seat. He noticed that today's hampers were suspiciously larger than the ones from the previous meetings.

After they all left, King Idris noticed that Abdulsalaam remained, he descended from the throne and went to sit with him.

"I don't remember you saying anything at the meeting, Abdul. I hope all is well with you," he said.

"I don't recall that you asked for my opinion," Abdulsalaam retorted.

"I threw the question to the floor. How did I not ask for your opinion?"

"Am I not supposed to be a little above the floor?" asked Abdulsalaam. "Must I learn of sensitive issues like this at the same time as everyone else?"

* * *

Abdulsalaam was King Idris's younger stepbrother. Just like Idris, Abdulsalaam was the only son his mother, the late Queen Halima, bore for the king. She passed away when Abdulsalaam was only a little boy, so Idris's mother, Queen Aisha, who was the first wife and queen mother of the empire, had taken in little Abdulsalaam as her own.

From the time they were children, Abdulsalaam was referred to by visitors to the palace as "the angry child." Despite this anger, Aisha treated Abdulsalaam the same as Idris. No one could understand the rage that shrouded Abdulsalaam. As a child, he fought his brother at the slightest provocation, and as he grew into a man, his rage became even worse, fueled, it seemed, by the knowledge that his older brother would become king someday.

Years ago, when the two princes had just returned from school in London, their father had called the family

Shadows of Exile

together and announced that Prince Idris was ready to be presented to the people of Mali as their next king. At the time, Idris had just graduated, while Abdulsalaam had one more year of studies left.

It was Idris's birthright as the first son to succeed his father, but according to tradition, the king could also choose someone else as his heir, as long as the person was from the royal bloodline. The kings of Mali had to observe their sons through the years to know which of them was most qualified to sit on the throne. If for any reason the ruling king thought his first son was not worthy of the throne, he could choose to make any of his other sons, any of his brothers' sons, or any other male from the royal bloodline the heir to his throne.

King Mustapha, however, had no reasons to pick any heir other than Idris. The boy had grown up gracefully to become like his father. He was intelligent and asked many questions that were beyond his age.

"His curiosity is my biggest pride," King Mustapha told his friends and councilmen each time Idris asked questions during one of their traditional functions.

As the day of the celebration approached, Abdulsalaam became obsessed with figuring out how he could get a shot at ascending the throne. He spent many sleepless nights and restless days weighing his options. *Should I poison him?* he wondered. *Should I pay people to assassinate him? Should I kill him in his sleep? Or should I frame him so Father will despise him?* So many possibilities came to mind, but none of them seemed easy to accomplish. Then he had an idea.

One day, emissaries from the Gold Coast of Ghana came to visit the king. Among the items they brought was a royal bracelet, intended as a sign of friendship after years of rivalry between the two kingdoms. Seeing that his father valued that bracelet very much, Abdulsalaam snuck into his father's room, stole the bracelet, and put it into Idris's jewelry collection.

As the day of Idris's presentation drew closer, Abdulsalaam held his breath, hoping that his father would start looking for the golden bracelet, but the king seemed so preoccupied with the arrangements that he didn't notice it was missing. So, on the day before the occasion, while King Mustapha was watching the servants decorate the banquet hall, Abdulsalaam approached him.

"Father," he said, and bent down on one knee.

The king tapped him on the shoulder, and he stood. Together, they began to admire the exquisite decorations.

"This is beautiful, don't you think?" the king asked, looking at his son expectantly, hoping to get an affirmation.

"It's artistically perfect, Father," Abdulsalaam concurred, "but I've come to you now not to admire the magnificent decorations, but instead to voice my concern for our kingdom."

"What concern?" the king asked, worry clear on his face.

"I fear that you might be making a decision you won't be able to correct or even realize needs correcting until it is too late."

"My son, those are deep words," the king said. "What do you think I'm doing wrong? Feel free to speak."

"Father, my tongue is tied. How can I speak ill against my blood?"

"Speak, Son. You are royalty. Your words are power. They shouldn't be hidden." Despite the king's urging, Abdulsalaam still hesitated.

"What's this about, Son? Speak to me. A wise man doesn't stay at home and watch the goat give birth with a rope around its neck. You can't watch us all make a mistake when you can correct it. Speak now! I command you."

"It's about my brother, Your Majesty."

"Your brother? What about him?"

"Don't you think you're moving too fast? Maybe you should take more time with him. Maybe there are things about him you need to correct before you give him that mantle." Abdulsalaam wore a sad look as he spoke. He chose his words carefully, making sure he didn't come across as desperate or malicious. He wanted his father to feel that he was speaking out of love for his family and the throne, not because he hated his brother.

"Are you saying that I don't know my son?" the king asked thoughtfully.

"Not that. But I think you may want to know my brother more. We lived together in London, so I know him better than anyone else. I'm just concerned about your legacy. Maybe you need to speak with him and teach him your ways. There are things he does that you may not be proud of, things that may bring shame to the throne someday."

"Tell me. How did Idris live in London? Did he deviate from our ways?" the king asked.

Though he did not let it show, the king was disappointed in Abdulsalaam. He knew everything about their stay in London just like he knew the palms of his own hands. His sons did not know that, even before they had left for London, he had sent many informants to watch them and make sure they didn't deviate from his principles. They didn't know that in their classes, in the streets, among their circle of friends, and even among the girls they dated, their father had informants and special guards. The king knew Abdulsalaam was trying to lie about his brother, but he allowed him to speak so he could catch him in his lies and chastise him.

"Father, he's my brother, but he has some habits that could bring shame to the throne. You may not be here to correct him when he embarrasses our family and our nation."

Abdulsalaam believed he had his father where he wanted him. He was going to tell him his brother was a thief. Then he would get king to look for his bracelet, and while he was doing so, Abdulsalaam would pay one of the servants to say he saw it in Idris's room. This would confirm his words, and the king would have no choice but to cancel the presentation.

He had it perfectly planned, but just as he was about to hammer the nail in, he heard Idris's voice as he walked into the banquet hall.

"Wow!" Idris exclaimed as he saw the decorations. "This is beautiful!"

The king turned around, and Idris walked up to them. He greeted the king and gave Abdulsalaam a friendly pat on the back. Idris was holding the golden bracelet.

"Father, I've been looking for you," he said, handing the bracelet to the king. "I saw this among my jewelry. You must be looking for it."

The king took the bracelet from Idris and clasped it over his wrist. "You said it was among your jewelry?"

"Yes. Maybe one of the servants misplaced it or something. I don't know," Idris said dismissively. He was still in awe of the gorgeous design of the room.

The king looked at Abdulsalaam suspiciously. Abdulsalaam cast his eyes to the floor. The king didn't need a soothsayer to tell him that Abdulsalaam was trying to set his brother up.

* * *

Now, many years later with both of them as grown men and Idris the king, Abdulsalaam still held resentment in his heart that their father had chosen Idris above him, that he had failed to rob his elder brother of his birthright.

Although he didn't always show his resentment, Abdulsalaam longed for everything Idris had. Even though he knew the kingdom's tradition, he still believed that Idris had stolen his life and he wanted it back by all means. He coveted the throne and craved for all the money and power Idris had as king. But above all else, he desired the love of the beautiful woman his brother had stolen from him.

Chapter Two

Shortly after Mallam Tanko and the other councilmen had left, King Idris observed his brother's countenance for a while and shook his head. "Brother, that isn't how it is. You're my only brother; your opinion matters to me, and you know it."

"There you lie. You're King Idris, king of kings and wisest of all men," Abdulsalaam retorted. He didn't bother hiding his sarcasm. "You don't need me. You've been so deafened and blinded by power that you won't realize it until it ruins you."

"Stop it, Abdulsalaam! Share your thoughts, but don't be abusive with words. I'm your elder brother and your king!"

"Then think like one. Think, Idris! You think this nonsense plan you have of giving everyone a share of the revenues from the gold is a good one? Is that your idea of equity? Equity is a mirage, Brother! It takes the bar a bit lower for a moment, but then it lifts it higher and makes riches turn to dust." Abdulsalaam's eyeballs popped out as he spoke, and a thick vein that ran across his forehead and disappeared just above his eyebrow pulsed.

As a man who loved power above everything else, Abdulsalaam hated to think that someday everyone in the kingdom would have wealth of their own. He wanted the entire wealth to remain and be controlled by their royal family, just as it had been in the days of their ancestors. At least that way, when he finally clinched power, the total wealth and fortune would flow into his purse. "It's good to know that you care. But look at the bigger picture, Brother. We will wipe away poverty in this land and all of the surrounding territories. Just try, please, to look at the bigger picture." The king smiled as he spoke. He wished he could open his brother's eyes and make him see the future he was trying to build. A future where every man would be able to provide for his family and afford to live a normal life. If only he had the power to paint that image in the darkened chamber of his brother's heart.

"Poor will be poor, and rich will be rich! That is the mystery of the universe. If every peasant in Mali—from Sikasso to Timbuktu and all the little nooks and crannies of this empire—can afford the good life, who then, would man your gates? Who would pour your juice? Who would hold this large double-edged sword and follow you around like a housefly lurking around a pile of dung?"

Abdulsalaam glanced at the palace guard standing beside the throne. The guard swallowed hard and looked the other way.

"Tell me, who? You think nature is a fool?"

King Idris waved at the servants to leave. They all exited the chambers, leaving just Idris and his brother.

Abdulsalaam continued his tirade. "You think you're wise, but your wisdom only takes you so far and deserts you when you need it most. Idris, don't you have respect for the throne on which you sit? Our gold belongs to the throne. Commoners have no place at the table of kings. It belongs to me and you! If you were wise, you would have spoken to me first before even thinking of making any peasant a shareholder to the king's table. You should have called me. We could have made these foreigners an offer that would keep us rich, that would raise us up so the commoners would have to look even higher into the skies before they could see us. But, no! You want to make everyone a shareholder, or gold-holder. How genius!"

Although King Idris was getting furious, he managed to keep his temper in check. For the sake of the family, he had learned over the years how to handle his brother. The only way to deal with an ambitious man like Abdulsalaam was to be very patient. He was not unaware of Abdulsalaam's envy, but he could not understand why he would have a problem with his plan to spread the wealth, especially because the plan wouldn't affect him negatively in any way. For a moment, King Idris tried to reason with his brother. He forced himself to imagine what could go wrong if poverty were wiped out in their land, but no matter how much he skewed his thoughts toward his brother's way of thinking, he couldn't make any sense of it.

"Our forefather, Mansa Musa I, shared gold bars with the poor. He gave their lives meaning and still remained the greatest king on Earth to date," Idris said, hoping this reminder would drown his brother's fear of living at the same level as a commoner.

Abdulsalaam laughed. "Oh, Idris, do I say that you forgot your history, or have you just twisted it to favor your half-baked, witless philosophies? Mansa Musa caused one of the biggest inflations the world has ever known. He made gold worthless. And he paid the price. The greatest king on Earth went borrowing. He knocked on the doors of moneylenders. What could be more demeaning to royalty?"

"Defame not the name of our forefather right under his roof, lest the grounds open up and swallow you!" King Idris blurted angrily. "Mansa Musa only borrowed to restore the economy. That was pure wisdom."

"And that wisdom is something you do not have!" Abdulsalaam retorted. "If you did, you would abort this foolish mission because you'll only create a monster you can't tame."

He stood and walked toward the exit. Then he turned back. "And don't ever compare yourself with Mansa Musa. He was everything you can never be!"

"Abdulsalaam! Abdulsalaam Mahmoud!" King Idris called.

But Abdulsalaam ignored him and walked away.

* * *

As soon as his chauffeur pulled into the main entrance of his palace, Abdulsalaam reached for the door and was out of the car before his servant, Ali, could get out of the passenger seat. Abdulsalaam walked hastily into the massive marble building, as angry as a wounded dog. He flung his hat onto the living room couch and strutted to the bar. He poured himself a glass of rum and gulped it down, his face squeezing into a frown as the hot sensation of the brown spirit hit his throat. Abdulsalaam's heart boiled with rage. He hated his brother now more than ever . How could he have underestimated his brother's foolishness? How could he have thought that his brother would be wise enough to accept the offer? When Abdulsalaam had planned this deal with the Chinese corporation, he had thought it was irresistible. He had wanted to simply remain in the background and watch his brother take the deal; a deal that would channel the billions into a single account that he would have complete access to when he eventually took over the throne.

"Ali!" he called to his servant, who was standing at the door of the living room. "Get Nkrumah on the phone! Tell him to hurry here immediately!" He added a few directives for the servant to pass on.

"Yes, my prince," Ali said, and pulled out his phone to call Nkrumah, one of the king's chief servants.

Nkrumah was Abdulsalaam's spy at his brother's royal palace. When Abdulsalaam had realized that his brother would not seek his consent before making decisions in the empire, he decided he needed to have someone who would keep him abreast of everything going on in the palace. One day, when a new batch of palace servants was posted to work at his palace, he caught Nkrumah answering a phone call at the back of the guards' quarters.

"Boil some *dogoyaro* leaves for her this morning, and then take her to the medicine man. I don't have money for a hospital, at least till the end of the month," Abdulsalaam overheard the servant saying into the phone.

Abdulsalaam then stepped out from where he was listening, and Nkrumah, upon seeing him, bowed.

"Greetings, my prince," he said, lowering himself onto one knee.

"Who was that?" Abdulsalaam asked.

"It was my sister," the humble servant replied.

"Is she ill?"

"No. My mother is sick. But I've asked my sister to take her to the medicine man. She'll be fine, Your Majesty."

"Why not take her to a hospital?" Abdulsalaam asked with a look of genuine concern on his face.

He couldn't take his mother to the hospital, Nkrumah explained, because he didn't have money, but he would do that when he received his salary.

Abdulsalaam saw his golden opportunity. He offered to fly Nkrumah's mother abroad for treatment, and he did. He also gave the servant money to establish a shop for his mother in the community market. Nkrumah was so grateful that he pledged his complete loyalty to Abdulsalaam, and since then, he had been at the prince's beck and call, telling him everything he needed to know about the king's palace. Initially, it had been nothing but petty things. But this was the day when Abdulsalaam would need Nkrumah to repay him.

* * *

It wasn't long before Nkrumah arrived. He was holding an envelope when he entered Abdulsalaam's study and closed the door behind him.

"Did you get me the papers?" Abdulsalaam asked. He stood beside the window smoking a cigar. Adjacent to him was a shelf stacked with books wrapped in old brown, blue, and black covers with different degrees of tear around the edges, the result of decades of continuous use. The titles of the books were written in Arabic—engraved deeply into the back covers in fading silver and gold.

"Yes, my prince," Nkrumah replied.

Abdulsalaam drew in a generous amount of tobacco, blew the smoke into the air, and walked to his seat. The smoke rose in circular rings behind him.

"Let me see," he commanded, and Nkrumah gave him the envelope.

Abdulsalaam opened the envelope and carefully checked the documents. There were land documents, account statements, and papers for several properties, both the ones his brother had acquired over the years and the ones that belonged to the family but were under the king's care. He read through the documents, pushed them back into the envelope, and dropped it on the table.

"Who would you say my brother trusts the most?" Abdulsalaam asked.

The question threw Nkrumah off-balance. He hadn't really seen the king acting particularly close to anyone apart from the queen and their two sons, Musa and Hamza.

"I don't understand, my prince. You know the king treats everyone the same way. Apart from the royal family, I can't really say that he's particularly close to anyone."

"You don't understand me," Abdulsalaam barked impatiently. "I mean among the servants. Who does he trust the most? Whose food does he eat instantly without the taster eating the food first?"

Nkrumah thought for a while. The king's taster was the king's shield. From the biggest bowl of chicken yassa to the tiniest bar of dark chocolate, the taster sampled every food before the king was allowed to partake. The king's guards stood at the door each time the king's food was brought, and they made sure that at no time did any food appear on the king's table without the taster—or even the cooks—having sampled it a few minutes earlier.

This same treatment applied to every cook in the palace, without any exceptions. Nkrumah couldn't think of any cook the king would trust so blindly. But then he remembered Alika, the king's butler.

King Idris could be said to trust Alika, not because he thought the butler could be trusted and others could not, but because unlike the cooks, Alika was always with the king. And Alika always had with him a bottle of royal fruit juice made specially for the king at the royal garden. Unlike the king's foods, the guards had no power over his juice. They couldn't call the taster to taste the drink before it was given to the king because the juice, made with grapes, apples, and other fruits from the royal garden, was strictly for the royal family. All others, including the tasters, were forbidden from ever drinking even a sip. Security around the royal garden was extremely tight.

"I think it would be Alika, the king's butler," Nkrumah said finally, breaking the silence. "The taster tastes everything the king eats, apart from his juice."

Having given his answer, Nkrumah wondered the reason Abdulsalaam asked the question. Before his suspicion could even take root, Abdulsalaam dropped the bombshell.

"Get me the king's butler. We have to know what his price is."

Nkrumah's heart pounded in his chest throughout the ride back to the palace. So many thoughts ran through his mind as it dawned on him that he may have sold his soul to the devil. If Prince Abdulsalaam wanted to know what the king eats and who gives it to him, could it mean he wanted to poison the king? Nkrumah shuddered at the thought of being part of a ploy to kill the king.

How could he even deliver the prince's message when he knew in his heart that it could make him a part of the grand conspiracy to kill the king? It was a scary thought to keep to himself. All he wanted to do was run to the king, fall on his feet, and confess all he had done. But his tongue was tied.

When he had sworn loyalty to Abdulsalaam, he had thought the only thing the prince wanted was to know what was happening in the palace. Now that he realized there was a greater price to pay than he had imagined, he cursed himself for not having asked questions in the beginning when Abdulsalaam had showered him with so much benevolence. He had been too naive, too greedy, and too stupid.

Months ago, after Abdulsalaam had paid Nkrumah's mother's hospital bills, he had called the servant and asked him how much he earned every month as a royal guard. When Nkrumah told him the amount he was being paid, the prince offered to pay him double his salary every month if he agreed to be his ears in the palace.

Abdulsalaam had also bought him a house and offered to send his children abroad to study when they reached college age. Blown away by the luxury of the lifestyle he was being offered, a lifestyle he could have only dreamt of, Nkrumah had said yes without asking anything. He had never stopped to wonder what important thing the prince could have wanted to know about the palace that he couldn't have known without the help of a mere servant.

* * *

The moment Nkrumah agreed to work for the prince, Abdulsalaam delivered the keys to the house and deposited twelve months of the agreed-upon salary into Nkrumah's bank account. Then, in the middle of the night, he took the servant to the banks of the sacred Sankarani River, where a fetish priest made him swear on a shallow mass grave where people who had drowned in the river many years ago were buried.

"If I ever betray the great Prince Abdulsalaam Mahmoud, tell the king about my conversations with him, or at any point decide that I will never work for him again, may I face the same fate as those on whose grave I swear this oath."

The priest brought out a white hen from the burlap sack hanging over his shoulder. He put a hand over the head of the hen, stifling the cry of the defenseless animal, which pierced the silence of the night. Then he squeezed the hen's neck and severed its head from the rest of its body.

The warm blood splashed all over Nkrumah's face and trickled down to his mouth. He snapped his eyes shut and squeezed his face in disgust as the metallic taste of the animal's blood touched his tongue. The priest then pointed the bleeding neck of the hen directly toward Nkrumah's head. The gushing blood poured onto the servant, the animal jerking back and forth as the last traces of life departed its body.

* * *

"God, what have I done?" Nkrumah cried as he parked the car in the garage reserved for the senior royal guards. If only he had known, he wouldn't have gotten himself in this position, but it was too late for regrets. He was bound to a covenant, and he must either fulfill his part of the agreement or pay the ultimate price.

Chapter Three

On the night when Abdulsalaam was to set off the chain of events that would change his destiny forever, he gave all the guards at his palace the night off. Alone, he waited for the representatives of the Chinese corporation to arrive. When they did, he took them up to the penthouse, where he planned to seal the deal with them in utmost secrecy. After they exchanged pleasantries and he offered them a drink, they began what would become an hour of back-and-forth debates. His patience waning, Abdulsalaam made his final offer. It was time to either sign the papers or find a more generous buyer.

"Three hundred billion dollars is so little to pay for fifty years," he said. "We can only give you twenty years, plus thirty percent royalties per annum. No more, no less."

The three foreigners excused themselves for a moment, moving to the window, where they talked in hushed tones a few steps from where Abdulsalaam sat. They then returned and took their seats.

"Twenty-five years," their spokesperson announced in a thick German accent.

Abdulsalaam watched the words spit from his mouth as if he had sucked in a flying insect by mistake. He thought for a while, but then agreed it was a fair arrangement. He would be sitting on that throne for more than twenty-five years anyway, so he would have more chances to milk this fat cow.

They signed the agreement, and then the spokesperson asked the three-hundred-billion-dollar question. "So what's your fastest route to the throne? We believe in a quick return on investment."

The man suggested they could help him with some "trusted hands," but Abdulsalaam told them not to worry. "I'll handle it from here," Abdulsalaam said, standing up and stretching out his hand for a goodbye handshake.

Abdulsalaam's plan was simple: poison the king and kill his sons in a car crash. He had it all figured out, and he had no thoughts of backing out, especially now that the deal had been signed.

He had waited all his life for this moment. He could already see himself sitting on that exalted throne, adorned with the kingly jewelries and the royal crown of Sikasso. The whole kingdom would gather in the city center to await the arrival of their newly crowned king. Then a limousine would pull over, and all eyes would turn to see him make his triumphant entrance. His royal orderly would open the door for him to step out of the limousine. As soon as his feet hit the ground, the whole crowd would bow in reverence to him. "Long live the king! Long live the king! Long live the king!" Their voices would echo as he walked towards his throne, placed on an elevated porch in the city's center. The tail end of his royal robe—a generously embroidered purple damask fabric laced with finely cut pieces of diamond and ruby—would sweep against the floor behind him as he walked graciously, two royal maidens dropping red and white roses for him to step on. As he arrived at his throne, he would gesture at the people to take their seats. Then he would look around him at the faces of his wives, his children, and his council of elders, all sitting in the front row. He would look at the smaller throne next to his. It would be vacant but beautifully decorated, as the kingdom would be expecting him to pronounce which of his wives would be the queen mother who would rule beside him. He would look at the faces of his wives again—from his first wife, Nana, who was his first love, the daughter of the former royal chef; to his last wife, Chidinma, a former Red Cross nurse he had met and fell in love with when he visited a refugee camp in Kigali. None of them would seem right for the throne, so he would stand and declare the grand reception canceled. A new date would be announced when his rightful queen was ready to be presented to the people—this time, not as a new queen but as an already sitting queen, no other woman qualified to take her place in the empire of the great King Abdulsalaam.

***

Alika did not know what to expect when he arrived at Abdulsalaam's house. Nkrumah had told him that Abdulsalaam wanted to see him, but he did not tell him the reason. When Alika had pressed him, Nkrumah said he didn't know for sure, but added that Abdulsalaam seemed angry and may have heard something bad about Alika and wanted to speak with him before reporting the issue to the king. Nkrumah had wanted to scare him as a way to keep him from telling anyone that he was going to the palace.

Alika barely slept that night. As soon as day broke, he hurried to Abdulsalaam's palace to hear the complaints made about him and to prove his innocence.

"Does the king know you're here?" Abdulsalaam asked as soon as he came out to meet Alika, who was waiting for him in his expansive living room.

"No, my prince," Alika replied.

Abdulsalaam smiled.

"My prince," Alika continued, "to the best of my knowledge, I have served the throne diligently from the day my father became too sick and handed the king's cup over to me. I promise that whatever you have learned must have been a misconception. Or maybe someone is trying to lie about me. I pray you will give me a chance to defend myself before you come to a conclusion."

This was exactly the kind of servants Abdulsalaam wanted to have around him the day he became king:

people who would search their hearts and not find a single time they had betrayed their master. In that moment, Abdulsalaam made up his mind to make Alika the head of all of the servants if he agreed to play ball.

"At ease, Alika!" Abdulsalaam cut in. "You've been a noble man, but your nobility hasn't gotten you much reward. How much would five million dollars change your life?"

"A lot," Alika blurted. He didn't repeat the figures the same way Nkrumah had done when Abdulsalaam made him his offer. "But I've never coveted such an amount of money or any money at all that isn't mine," Alika continued in his defense, still wondering what his crime could be.

"I will give you ten million dollars as a token for a little job. Once the job is done, I will pay you another twenty million dollars and give you two houses, one in Bamako and one in Timbuktu," Abdulsalaam countered.

"My prince, what kind of job would make you give me such a fortune?" the butler asked, seemingly unimpressed.

"I will give you something to slip into my brother's drink," Abdulsalaam whispered while staring directly into Alika's eyes.

Alika cringed and jumped from the seat. "Sacrilege!" he screamed.

"Hey! Calm down! All you need to do is put a pinch of it into his glass and pour his juice. He would join our ancestors in the great beyond, and the substance would never be traceable in his system, so poisoning would be ruled out completely."

"Say no more!" Alika barked, his voice echoing loudly like an angry father chastising a naughty child.

Abdulsalaam's eyes protruded in shock. No one had spoken to him that way since his father had died, not even his brother, the king. He could have gotten furious and ordered his guards to throw him into the dogs' cage—as he had done to Bashiru, the young interior designer who had been hired to change the chandeliers in Abdulsalaam's daughter's bedroom and was caught chatting and smiling with the teenage girl, who had just returned from high school in Scotland.

Abdulsalaam tried to be patient with Alika. He doubled the money and the number of houses and was willing to add even more, but the servant stood up and stormed out on him. Alika jumped into his car and quickly drove off.

Driving furiously down the main road, Alika saw some boys trying to push a broken-down vehicle off the road. He waited in the car and honked for them to move the car away so he could drive past, but they kept stalling. Impatient, he got out of the car and went to ask why all four of them couldn't push a single vehicle, but before he could finish his question, a heavy blow landed on the bridge of his nose, and the only thing he saw before everything disappeared into darkness was a thick sack being pulled over his face.

Back in his palace, Abdulsalaam's phone beeped as a text came in. He picked up the phone and read the text: "Done!"

He deleted the text and dialed another number. "I think I should take you up on that offer."

Chapter Four

It was a cool evening in Sikasso. The chirping sound of birds in the garden sweetly pierced the solemn silence of the royal palace. The gate opened from time to time for a car or two to drive in as guests and subjects came to commune with the king.

As the evening crawled into night, King Idris's oldest son, Musa, who was named after his great ancestor, Mansa Musa I, sat on his bed scripting ideas for a novel. Menkiti, one of the royal servants, who Musa particularly enjoyed talking to, had told him the story of a young woman who was a victim of a house fire in his village many years ago. The woman was just a little girl when the incident happened. She watched her parents and siblings roast in the raging inferno, but by some lucky twist of fate, she was able to run into the bathtub, where she stayed until help came.

The girl was rescued from the fire, but it left indelible scars on her body and singed off all of her hair. Over the years, she kept praying for at least a strand of hair to sprout from her scalp. She lived the life of a loner because nobody wanted to be close to a girl scarred from head to toe. Strangers who had no idea of what she had been through stared at her in disgust each time she walked past. She lived in pain, agony, shame, and self-hate until she couldn't take it anymore, until she finally did the unthinkable.

Musa was astounded when Menkiti told him the story. He had thought about this woman all day and had so many questions. What if she had held on to life a little longer? What if she had found love? What if she had found a person who would love her more than anything else in the world? What if she had found a person who would accept her and embrace her differences, and together they could show off the beautiful love they shared without a care in the world?

Musa took it upon himself to rewrite her story. He would write a beautiful love story of the way her life should have turned out. Musa had always wanted to be a writer. He planned to write two novels every year until he graduated from the university. He was currently on break halfway through his sophomore year, and he hoped that he would complete the story before the break ended. That way, he could send the manuscript to a publisher once he got back to Oxford.

As Musa poured his heart into the story, his younger brother, Hamza, opened the door and walked in, waving a printed flyer.

"Musa, did you know that this year's Love Music Fest will be held in Dubai?" Hamza asked. He jumped onto the bed, placing the flyer over Musa's keyboard.

"Oh, this boy!" Musa sighed.

He had planned to lock himself inside his room—the only way he would meet his target without Hamza's disturbance, but the excitement of the story had made him forget to lock the door when he entered. "Yeah, I heard it on the news last night. It's starting on Saturday."

"Dang! I'm already bored to the bones here. Let's go and have some fun this weekend," Hamza said.

"No, no." Musa shook his head. "I can't afford that luxury now. I need to crack this story. And remember we should visit the IDP refugee camp on Monday. Dad said the medical facility there is a total disaster. He has ordered new equipment that we'll be donating to them. So, this weekend is out."

"Come on, big bro. You can write anywhere in the world. And we can visit the IDP camp when we return. Tuesday is fine. Let's just have some fun this weekend. Don't be a party pooper," Hamza teased Musa.

"Hamza, just go alone. I'll come with you some other time. Right now, I have to throw myself into this story. We can go to the IDP camp when you come back, but this story has got my weekend."

"You know Dad won't let me go if you aren't there. Come on, Bro. Michael Jackson is gonna be there. Prince, The Backstreet Boys, and other top entertainers Do you really want to miss that?"

Hamza kept pressing till Musa gave in, but Musa made Hamza promise that he wouldn't disturb him anytime he picked up his computer to write.

"I cross my heart!" Hamza said, and flashed a dimpled grin—the victory smile he wore each time he schemed someone into doing things his way.

Despite their mother's complaint that they hadn't been home for long, their dad agreed to let them go. The boys returned to Musa's room, then Hamza started typing a text to send to the family pilot to arrange their trip.

* * *

When Nkrumah went all day without seeing Alika, he feared that the worst had happened to him. He should have warned Abdulsalaam that Alika's loyalty was as deep as a bottomless pit.

"What if Alika said no to the prince and still managed to escape?" he wondered.

That would mean great danger for him because Alika would lay everything bare before King Idris, and he, Nkrumah, would be in big trouble. He shuddered as he imagined the wrath he would face if this got to the king. He prayed Alika wouldn't make it out of Abdulsalaam's palace. He prayed they had killed him if he had failed to play along.

Immediately, Nkrumah felt disappointed in himself. He never would have believed that he would wish death on a fellow man. "What have I gotten myself into?" he cried.

Just then, his phone beeped. It was a text from Abdulsalaam: "Don't sleep in the palace tonight."

At that point, Nkrumah had no doubt that Alika was either dead or being held captive somewhere and something terrible was going to happen. As the night drew closer, Nkrumah called Khadija to meet him in his room. Khadija was one of the palace maids in charge of the queen's manicures. She entered the room, closed the door, and leaned on it, holding the knob behind her and smiling seductively at Nkrumah, who was sitting on the bed.

"You naughty boy!" she said. "It's not even been twenty-four hours and you're already yearning for more. Hmmm?"

She walked up to him, pushed him gently onto the mattress, and started kissing him. Nkrumah returned her kisses gently as he tried to figure out the best way to tell her that they both needed to stay out of the palace that night.

"Hey, I want to propose something," he said in between their kisses.

"Okay?"

"How about we try something new?"

"Like what?" she asked.

"Like sleeping outside of the palace tonight. We'll stay somewhere nice and knock ourselves out from sunset to sunrise."

Khadija jumped at the offer. She was in for anything that smelled of sex.

Nkrumah planned to marry her someday, but what he did not know was that right after she snuck out of his room the night before, she snuck into the room of the electrician, Bala, to satisfy the craving that he could not tame in the two minutes and forty seconds they were together. He jerked in and out of her before screaming like a dying goat as he filled her with warm droplets of his sticky seed.

* * *

Abdulsalaam met the hit men at an old warehouse north of Sikasso. There were twenty-four of them—huge men with unsmiling faces, arms as thick as tree trunks, and hefty chests. Abdulsalaam had told his accomplices the palace was always swarmed with guards, so they decided it would be best to send two dozen special squads trained at a secret military facility in Russia.

They gathered around a table and watched as Abdulsalaam spread the blueprint of the palace on the table.

"The men at this spot have to act first. To deactivate the electric fencing, all you need to cut is the yellow wire you'll find in a black box on the wall here." He pointed at the sketches as he explained. "There are nine wires all together clustered at the lower right corner. If you mistakenly cut any other wire apart from the yellow one, you'll trigger the alarm system and you'll be compromised.

There's a black wire in the center. It's quite prominent; don't touch it. It's sensitive to touch, and a counter records how many times you touch it. Four touches in less than one minute and a sophisticated lockdown initiates, turning the palace into a fortress no army can penetrate." He looked up at their faces to make sure they understood him perfectly. They all stared at him like morons.

"Do you understand?" he barked.

"Yes, sir!" they replied.

Abdulsalaam could guess what was going on in their minds. Most of them could not believe that a palace in Africa could be so large with such sophisticated security.

He divided them into groups and assigned them to different corners of the palace from where they would invade the building once they got the message that the fence had been deactivated.

"I will need two people to follow me through this secret entrance," Abdulsalaam said, pointing at a tower some distance from the palace. "We will enter before the rest of you."

"You'll get there before the security is deactivated?" one of the hit men asked.

"Yes. Its security system differs from the rest of the palace's. It uses passcodes only."

This secret entrance led to the king's bedroom. It began at the ramparts of an abandoned city tower behind the palace and opened behind a wall that looked like a bookshelf inside the king's room. It was built for the escape of the king and his family in times of danger, and only the kings and their sons were allowed to know about it. Their father had shown them the exit when they had grown into adults.

As far as Abdulsalaam knew, only King Idris and he knew about the entrance. He was sure that his brother hadn't shown his sons the tunnel; after all, they were still teenagers, and there had been no threats or any other reason so far for their father to show them any of the secret exits in the palace.

Abdulsalaam paused for a moment to decide whether he should say what he was about to share. There was yet another secret entrance through a tunnel behind the engine room. It had neither a code nor an electric security system. He decided it would be unwise to tell them. With a big enough paycheck from an enemy in the years to come, these same hit men might be the ones to storm his palace and take his life.

He went over the instructions again, just to be sure everyone understood him. He warned them not to mess this deal up, as the stakes were very high. It must be a clean job because he was putting his identity on the line, and any mistakes would be the end of him.

They loaded their weapons and drowned their souls in liquor as they waited for the night to approach to unleash terror on the royal palace.

Chapter Five

For Menkiti, it all started with a blur. His head had been spinning all day, and he was only able to get some sleep after taking the hot and bitter *dogoyaro* concoction that Hadiza, the medicine woman, prepared and gave his sister to bring him. The king's doctors had been giving him tablets for the past two days, but he only took one dose and threw the rest under the mattress.

Menkiti heard a heavy thud as he entered the bathroom to relieve himself. It was followed by another thud and yet another one. Menkiti held his groin muscles to stop the sound of his urine pouring into the toilet. He listened carefully and heard another thud, and then the sound of footsteps approaching the building. He zipped up his trousers, climbed on the toilet seat, and peeked through the glass window. He froze as he saw four tall and hefty men standing by the fence behind the palace. A fifth man jumped down from the fence and cocked his gun—a long, black Uzi that shimmered under the bright white halogen lights around the fence. He fixed a silencer to the tip of his gun, screwed it tight, and hurried to join the squad.

"How did this armed man get past the electric ropes on top of the fence?" Menkiti wondered.

Menkiti jumped down and hurried out of the bath-room to alert the security guards. He ran down the hall-way and rushed to the front door. He peered through the keyhole and saw nine security guards lying on the floor. Their hands were stretched out above their heads, and they were shaking like the dried leaves of a baobab tree dancing in a harsh *harmattan* wind. Seven armed men were standing above them, pointing their guns at them.

"Move it!" a voice shouted.

The door of the security post tore open, and one of the intruders dragged out Audu, the chief security officer. Audu landed on his belly and gave out a loud grunt.

"We don't have time!" one of the intruders said in a strange accent and shot at the men lying helplessly on the floor. "Where are the others?" he barked.

"Some went through the back fence," one of the in-truders replied, pointing, "and the rest should be inside with the boss by now."

Menkiti ran back into the palace as the men ap-proached the front door. He wondered if he should scream to wake everyone in the palace or run to the king's cham-bers and tell him what was going on. The hallway was long, and he knew that the armed men would get inside soon. As he ran, he tried the knobs of all the doors he passed, but they were all locked. He heard the front door opening, so he slammed himself against the nearest door, and it crashed open.

A sleepy Sadiya, one of the maids, jerked up from her sleep.

"What are you doing here?" she asked.

"Shh. Keep your voice down!" Menkiti said in a whisper as he closed the door behind him. He placed his ear against the door and listened for footsteps, but the intruders seemed to be very far down the hallway.

Sadiya started backing toward the wall, wondering what Menkiti had up his sleeves as he drew closer to her.

"If you do anything stupid, I will shout!" she threatened.

"Keep quiet and listen to me! We are under attack. Some armed men just entered the palace, and they have killed the guards at the gate."

Sadiya's heart sank. She started panicking.

"What are we going to do?" she cried.

"Hide under your bed. I'm going to get the princes. I don't know if the guards at their doors are awake."

As Sadiya struggled to squeeze under her bed, Menkiti climbed up the wardrobe, lifted the vent on the ceiling, and entered the ducts that ran throughout the attic. At first, he felt like he was going to suffocate in the heat and stale air, but he held his breath and allowed his eyes to adjust to the darkness, then began moving. As he crawled through the ducts, he could hear people below him crying and begging for their lives.

Menkiti had been in the ducts many times before to clean them, so it was easy for him to trace his way to Musa's room. As soon as he lowered himself into the room, he tiptoed to Musa's bed. Luckily, Hamza was sleeping beside him. "Musa, Hamza, wake up!"

Musa and Hamza opened their eyes and yawned. Menkiti rushed to the door, locked it, and returned to the boys.

"Hey, we have to escape now. The palace is under attack. They're killing everyone."

"Why? What are you saying? Who is killing?" Musa stammered.

"I don't know. And there's no time for questions," Menkiti snapped as he paced around looking for an escape route.

He slid the glass window to the side and tore the mosquito net.

"Let's go through the back to His Majesty's room," he said as he looked out through the torn net and found the area clear. He jumped out, and Musa and Hamza followed him.

Shouts and wailing filled the palace as gunshots flew from all corners. Menkiti and the boys hunched over and tiptoed through the backyard to the window of the king's room.

Menkiti and Musa peeked into the room through a crack between the thick window curtains of the king's room, while Hamza, scared to his bones, hung behind them. As the fog from Menkiti's warm breath cleared, they saw a familiar figure, Abdulsalaam, standing over the king with a revolver in his hand. Their mouths fell open in shock.

The king was kneeling on the floor, begging for his life, while his brother waved the revolver angrily in his face. They looked around and saw the queen lying in a pool of her own blood. Musa opened his mouth to scream, and Menkiti instinctively put his hand over the boy's mouth.

"You want everything to go your way! It's always been all about you. You alone! From birth, our lives have revolved around doing what you wished."

"Abdul! It's not just about what I want. It's about our legacy, our commonwealth. These people just want to get their hands on our wealth, use us to enrich themselves, and render us all poor. Have you forgotten everything you read about colonialism? Please don't let them use you!"

"Keep quiet, you greedy monster! You've ruled the Kingdom of Mali for twenty years, and what do we get? Tyranny! And you have managed to brainwash everyone into thinking that you're the best thing that has happened to this kingdom since Mansa Musa. But it's over. Pass on my greetings to Mom and Dad; tell them that I've come to give Mali the kind of leadership they envisioned for it."

He tightened his grip on the gun and pointed it at the king's head.

"Abdul, please! Please don't do this!" the king pleaded, but Abdul pulled the trigger repeatedly, lodging seven bullets in his brother's skull.

Menkiti pulled Musa and Hamza away from the window, trying to calm them and quiet their sobs. They heard Abdulsalaam's voice roar inside the house. "Get the boys. Don't let any soul escape; not even an ant!"

"Shh. Musa, get a grip on yourself, we have to escape now," Menkiti said.

"How will we do that? The whole palace is swarmed," Musa said. "Just follow me. There is a secret tunnel behind the engine room. If we can make it to the engine room without being caught, we should be able to get out of here alive." Menkiti grabbed the boys by their hands, and they raced toward the engine room at the west wing of the chaotic palace.

Menkiti was the only servant who knew about the tunnel. He had been inside it once many years ago as a young boy while accompanying his father, a palace worker who had long since passed away. Menkiti hadn't been inside it since then, but he could still remember how to navigate to the outside. The tunnel was pitch black and had no lights, so there was no way for an enemy to find it.

"I can't see anything! How are we supposed to go through this darkness?" Hamza asked as the darkness inside the tunnel enveloped them.

"Shh. Hold on to my hand," Menkiti said. "We need to be as quiet as possible. Just walk with me, we will see the light soon."

"But how did you know about this place? Our father never showed it to us," he said.

"My father showed me once," Menkiti replied.

"Your father showed you a royal secret?" Hamza snapped.

"I was only a little boy and my mother had just died, and so my father had no choice but to take me to live with him in the palace. One day, your grandfather sent him to clean up this tunnel after a heavy flood hit the city. He trusted my father with that secret, and I think it was destiny that made me cry so much that day that he had no choice but to take me along to stay with him while he worked," Menkiti explained.

* * *

In the palace, two hit men crashed through the doors of Musa's and Hamza's rooms. Hamza's room was empty, and in Musa's room they saw the open roof and torn window net.

"Shit! They escaped!"

They growled in disappointment and rushed to the king's room to tell Abdulsalaam, who was scrambling through the papers in the wardrobe.

"The boys escaped," one of them announced.

"What? How? How the hell did that happen?"

"We saw an open roof and a torn window net. They either escaped from the roof or through the torn net."

Abdulsalaam was furious. He ordered some of the men to climb to the roof to check and others to search the rest of the rooms in the palace.

"Damn! Damn!" he yelled.

Then it hit him. They must have escaped through the tunnel. Could his brother have already shown it to them? He wondered if he should take some men and go into the tunnel to look for the boys himself, but he shook his head. "No, these guys are not to be trusted."

Instead he pulled out his phone and made a call. Somewhere in an exotic hotel, a sleep-deprived Nkrumah jerked up from the bed as the sound of his ringtone pierced the night. He looked at Khadija, who was snoring lightly beside him, and then picked up the phone and went to the bathroom.

"Your Majesty."

"Nkrumah, drive to Asante Riverside. You'll see some men in a red Toyota parked at the entrance of the Riverside Market. Tell them you're the one. You'll help them identify Musa and Hamza."

"They escaped?" Nkrumah blurted in shock.

Abdulsalaam paused for a moment. "Yes," he said, "and you're the only one who can help me find them."

Chapter Six

Menkiti and the boys walked through the dark tunnel for almost two hours before they saw a tiny shaft of light peeking through. Having walked blindly for so long, their eyes hurt as more rays of light shone into the tunnel. Then, finally, the tunnel opened into a hall packed with old carvings and molded sculptures of long bearded Islamic clerics, with a series of Arabic inscriptions written on its walls. The air in the room was stuffy and everything was covered in a thick layer of dust.

"Where are we?" Hamza asked, taking stock of the odd items around him. It looked like a museum. Hamza hated carvings and artifacts. He always found them creepy. The last and final time he had visited a museum was three years ago when his family had gone on vacation to Egypt and gone to see the Egyptian mummies.

Hamza had been scared to learn that the mummies had been humans who had died many centuries ago. He feared that the mummies would resurrect, turn off the lights, and kill everyone in the building. He remembered a movie he had seen as a little boy where tourists went to a museum to take pictures of the mummies and suddenly the mummies mystically took over the tourists' bodies, using them to cover their own desiccated bodies and leaving the humans with only skeletons. He threw up twice inside the museum and had nightmares for two weeks before he could get over the horror that assailed his imagination.

"My father said it used to be the imams' court," Menkiti explained. "During the reign of Mansa Musa, he propagated the growth and spread of Islam so much that imams from different parts of the world came to Mali to worship with and bless the mansa for being Allah's great tool. Some of the imams fell in love with the land and decided to stay and help Mansa Musa build the place into the dreamland we have today. So, Mansa Musa built a special mosque for the imams at Asante Riverside. People went there to seek counsel and prayers from the imams, but this particular room was kept secret, and only the clerics and the king were allowed into it."

They kept quiet and listened carefully for the sound of footsteps coming from the tunnel, but there was none. They climbed a flight of stairs built with mud and bamboo sticks, which led them into the main mosque. A part of it had collapsed over the years, and thick bushes had grown around it. Only a few walls were still standing, and a mammoth crowd of insects was climbing up and down their cracked edges. Around the collapsed building were trees filled with nests, and birds flew in and out of them, chirping excitedly as they basked in the morning sun. It was clear to Menkiti and the boys that the building had been deserted for centuries.

Cautiously they squeezed their way out of the ruins and onto a small rock in front of the building overlooking the Asante River. The boys sat down. They were exhausted and traumatized. It still felt like a very bad dream. Musa could not believe that he just saw his uncle murder his father. Rage boiled deep inside him. He clenched his fist, rubbed his eyes, and started to slap himself.

"Musa, wake up! Wake up! Wake up from this nightmare," he screamed. He was on the verge of hysteria.

Menkiti grasped him on both shoulders and shook him vigorously. "Musa! Get a grip. This is not a dream. And this is not the time to freak out. Don't draw attention to this place, because everyone you see here might be your enemy."

He hugged the boy tightly and allowed him to weep for some minutes.

"You need to be a man now, Musa. If you start crying, how do you expect Hamza to be strong? This is your destiny. If it weren't, you wouldn't be alive now."

Musa stood up and took some moments to gather his strength and face the reality before him. It was market day in Asante Town. From the rock where he stood, he could see canoes and speedboats hurrying toward the riverbank; traders from neighboring towns were coming to buy and sell goods.

"Where do we go from here?" Musa asked.

"We need to get you both to safety first," Menkiti replied. He was deep in thought, wondering who he could trust with the safety of the boys. He was sure that apart from the assassins who had invaded the palace, Abdulsalaam must have had people working inside the palace, people who the king had entrusted with the safety of his family, who had helped Abdulsalaam carry out his monstrous scheme.

So many names came to his mind, but he had a hard time convincing himself that anyone was trustworthy. He thought of the councilmen; they were the best people to seek justice for the boys and the slain king and the queen, but which of them could he turn to?

He remembered the way those men smiled each time they were given hampers at the palace or whenever the king decided to give them brown envelopes stuffed with crisp minted dollars or pounds sterling. No, they would be the worst people to turn to in a time like this. For the right amount of money, those men would sell the boys to their uncle.

"We need to cross over to Banfora and stay for a few days while we figure out a safer place to go."

"Banfora?" the boys exclaimed in unison.

"Yes."

Musa cast him a suspicious glance. "Do you realize that Banfora is the worst enemy of the throne of Sikasso?"

"Yes, sometimes you're better off having your enemies around you than the people you think are your friends."

"This is like suicide. How can we escape murder only to surrender ourselves into the hands of our age-old enemies who would give the lives of a thousand of their people if that's what it took to see one of us get hurt?" Musa snapped angrily.

"Did you see that massacre? That was your uncle. The man was supposed to be like a father to you. He's the person you were supposed to trust most after your parents and little brother. Did you see how thirsty he was for your blood? That's how the people you call friends sometimes behave. Their eyes are always on you. They're given to jealousy and can easily turn into enemies." Menkiti scolded the boys and convinced them to trust him, to follow his lead and not be scared.

They needed to get to the riverbank and board a boat, but they had no money on them. Menkiti asked them to wait for him and not go anywhere. He went down to the market. Some traders were busy displaying their wares in front of their stalls, while others were struggling to get a spot in the open trade zones, where clothing and shoe sellers displayed their goods by heaping them on a polythene carpet.

There was a small queue at the ATM machine in front of a commercial bank beside the market. Menkiti did not have an ATM card on him, so he needed to wait until eight o'clock when the banks would open their doors to allow customers into the banking hall.

He sat on the paved floor in front of the security post and waited, when suddenly something caught his eye. He saw Nkrumah talking with some strange-looking men beside a red Toyota parked under a tree close to the riverside. Nkrumah was speaking and gesticulating with both hands. His hands moved from his face to his shoulders, like he was trying to describe the physical features of a person.

Menkiti did not need a priest to tell him that his suspicion was right. Nkrumah must be working with Abdulsalaam, and if they were there, it meant that Abdulsalaam suspected that the boys had escaped through the tunnel. Though if that were so, Menkiti wondered why they had not come after them when they ran into the tunnel. He needed to get the boys away from there before the killers could locate them.

Menkiti's mind ran far and wide, wondering what to do. They needed money, but right now he couldn't sit and wait for the bank to open. He wondered if he should beg someone to give him some money. No, that was a bad idea. That might draw attention to him, and it was too early for anyone to give money to a stranger.

He looked around and saw some clothes hung on clotheslines inside a native compound opposite the bank. Menkiti crossed to the other side of the road and cautiously walked to the clotheslines. He quickly grabbed some clothes and hurried away, his eyes darting this way and that, checking to see if anyone had seen him.

On his way back to the rock, Menkiti picked up a jute bag and an oil-stained plastic container he found at the back of a stall. He hurried to the rocks and met the boys where he had left them.

"We need to get out of here now," he announced, and gave them the stolen clothes. "Some of the hit men are down at the riverside. They know we are here, so we need to disguise ourselves as much as possible and get out of here before they find us."

The boys slipped on the clothes—ankle-length galabiyas faded from years of merciless use by the owners—over the ones they already had on. Menkiti helped them wrap the turbans around their heads in such a way that no one would recognize them.

"Did you get the money?" Musa asked. "I couldn't. But let's ransack the mosque. We might be lucky and find something."

"Hasn't it been decades since anyone used this mosque?" Hamza asked.

"Yes, but this is Mansa Musa's mosque. You never can tell what you'll find." Menkiti began to unpack some old wooden seats clustered at one corner, hoping to find something valuable.

"You really think that because it's Mansa Musa's mosque, we might find something here even after all this time?" Hamza pressed Menkiti.

Menkiti ignored him and continued his search. Then he saw an old box with rusty hinges and a small lock.

"I think I found something," he announced.

The boys drew closer. Menkiti hit the hinges a few times with a piece of rock, and it broke apart, allowing him to open the box. Inside were a few stacks of the old West African CFA, a currency which had been phased out many years ago. His face fell in disappointment, but then under the stack of money, Menkiti found two old, rough-looking gold bars and an old necklace laced with dust. He pulled them out.

"What are those?" Musa asked.

"What do they look like?" Menkiti scoffed.

"Those are gold bars, Mansa Musa's gold bars! Gracious goodness!" Musa exclaimed, reaching out to touch the rough pieces of metal.

Menkiti gave the boys one bar each to hide in their pockets and wiped the dirt off the necklace before putting it around his neck. They filled a bag with grass, sticks, and every other light object they could lay their hands on. Hamza carried it on his head, while Musa bore a rubber container. Then Menkiti, disguised to look like an old man, cut down a tree branch to use as a cane.

They discreetly walked out onto the road, looking like an old man running errands with his grandchildren. Menkiti did not tell the boys about the red Toyota, so they didn't flinch or even notice Nkrumah and the hit men, who were still lurking there as they walked past.

At the river, Menkiti saw a speed boat waiting for its turn to load new passengers, so he approached the driver and asked, "Banfora?"

The man shook his head. Banfora wasn't a regular route. It would take a lot of time to get a handful of people going to Banfora, so the sailors did not like to ply that route.

"Banfora," Menkiti shouted again.

"One thousand," the man announced, trying to discourage him with the outrageous price.

There was no time to negotiate with the man or to remind him that the highest price any boat charged to Banfora was 400 CFA. Instead, Menkiti boarded the boat and then helped the boys on. "No problem. Let's go. We are running late."

"I said one thousand!" the sailor repeated.

"I heard you the first time. You know one thousand is too much, but let's go. We need to get to Banfora right away."

"When we get there, you give me one thousand. I don't want trouble." The sailor reiterated his price again before he reluctantly turned on the engine and sped off, with Menkiti watching Nkrumah and the hit men roam the area like a hungry pack of wolves

"How could you, Nkrumah? How could you?" he thought.

Chapter Seven

The journey from Asante to Banfora took almost an hour. Musa and Hamza reflected on the traumatic events of the morning. "So this is real?" Musa thought. He kept his eyes fixed on the ripples on the surface of the river that formed as the blades of the speeding boat sliced their way through the waters.

He wondered what death was really all about. *Does it mean that Mom and Dad have been sent away from the Earth, to another world, or does it all end here? Is there really life after death, or are those just illusions religious leaders cook up to hold their followers spellbound? Are they just stories to make people believe that even if their lives on earth aren't as good as they would like them to be, they'll get another chance in a world where nature isn't so cruel?*

If there was anything like the supernatural, Musa would give anything to transcend to that realm now; to ask his father for some explanation that could help him make sense of the tragedy that had befallen them. He had never seen his uncle as someone who would ever hurt anyone. He had overheard his father and uncle arguing about one issue or the other, but no sooner than he heard their raised voices would the cackling sound of their laughter fill the room. Musa could not have imagined that his uncle would hurt them. He remembered all the times their uncle took them on family picnics. As king, their father would sometimes be too busy to go with them, but Uncle Abdulsalaam would always be available to go with them and their mother to the park, zoo, or anywhere else they wanted to go to. Uncle Abdulsalaam was a giver, at least to the royal family. Musa could still remember that it was Abdulsalaam who, on his last birthday, gifted him the laptop computer he used to write his story just the night before. Although he had another personal computer, he cherished the one Uncle Abdulsalaam gave him more, not only because it had a bigger screen and keyboard, but because of the words his uncle had written on a note attached to the golden nylon foil with which the present was wrapped: "To my favorite nephew, the young writer in whose written pages the world will someday see the light."

Musa looked at Hamza, who had dozed off against the wooden wall of the boat and prayed for the strength to protect and take care of him. There were so many questions running through his mind, many of which he knew he would never get answers to, some of which he knew time would tell, and one that needed an immediate answer: What was Menkiti's plan?

* * *

Shadows of Exile

According to the stories King Idris had told Musa, Banfora used to be one of the numerous allies of the great empire of Mali. In the olden days, even before the times of the great Mansa Musa I, the empire of Mali was very powerful and vast. When Mansa Musa I became king, many more kingdoms were conquered, and his empire spanned through the modern-day countries of Senegal, southern Mauritania, Mali, northern Burkina Faso, western Niger, Guinea-Bissau, Guinea, the Ivory Coast, northern Ghana, and the Gambia. Because of Mansa Musa I, the empire of Mali became both the place every other part of Africa looked up to and the place they feared.

Unlike other kingdoms that went to war, Banfora was just a small village made up of hunters, farmers, and fishermen. Banfora was peaceful; they had no ax to grind with any kingdom. The people of Banfora always stayed within the bounds of their land, only crossing their borders to go to other villages on market days to sell their goods and buy the things they needed. They didn't have any need for warriors; they hoped that their lives would continue to be as peaceful as they had always been, so they made no preparations for warfare.

One day, a swarm of fishermen from Dakota, a land of warriors, stormed Banfora's rivers and chased all of the local fishermen away. The intruders took over the river, and the people of Banfora couldn't fight back because they stood no chance against the mighty warriors of Dakota, who had defeated all of the lands around them and were even threatening to challenge Mansa Musa's Malian empire.

The river, however, wasn't enough for the Dakotans. One night, they stormed the kingdom and slaughtered the people like animals who were unable to flee. The aggrieved king of Banfora looked to the hills, mountains, and deserts, but he couldn't see any hope of reclaiming his kingdom or avenging the death of his people. The king ran to Mansa Musa I to seek help.

"Save my people, oh king of kings," the troubled king cried as he prostrated at the feet of Mansa Musa.

Mansa Musa looked around at the servants and guards surrounding him. "Leave us!" he commanded, and they left. He held the other king's hand and helped him to his feet.

"Kings don't cry, and kings don't bow to anyone, at least not in front of commoners," Mansa Musa chastised him.

"A king is a man who has a kingdom to rule. I have lost my kingdom, so what makes me a king?"

"Royalty flows in the blood and not on the throne. If there's no royalty, there's no throne. Get up, my friend, and tell me what troubles you."

The Banforan king poured his heart out to Mansa Musa. As he narrated his ordeal, Mansa Musa nodded his head in sympathy. Finally, he had an opportunity to

Shadows of Exile

put the Dakotans in their rightful place. He had heard numerous threats of war against his empire, but he was not an impulsive king who would fire the first arrow. Instead he waited for the Dakotans to step on the feet of his people first—even if it was something as seemingly insignificant as spilling the wine of the poorest palm wine tapper in Mali or going to war with any of his allies.

"What do you want me to do for you?" Mansa Musa asked after the Banforan king had narrated his story.

"I need you to help me fight and get my kingdom back."

"Where are your people now? The ones who survived."

"They are hiding in a cave near the Tsigali Desert," the Banforan king said.

"Bring them here and let them have a good place to rest; for by this time tomorrow, they will all be dancing on the severed heads of the strongest warriors of Dakota."

Mansa Musa dispatched ten thousand-foot soldiers to Banfora and another ten thousand to Dakota. The soldiers stormed the land of Dakota and killed the Dakotans in droves until the few surviving ones surrendered. In Banfora, no single Dakotan was spared. In accordance with the command of Mansa Musa, the soldiers continued their attack until the bloods of the Dakotans washed the land they had desecrated. As Mansa Musa had promised the Banforan king, the next day there was great jubilation in Banfora as the Banforans saw the corpses of their enemies lined up along the roadside. They got back their lands, their river, and everything they had lost.

In his benevolence, Mansa Musa handed over Dakota to the Banforan king. "I have no need for their land," Mansa Musa said. "It wasn't my war. It was yours. I was only a helper, and I don't think a helper in times of war should be the one to enjoy the spoils of war. They are your slaves, do with them as you please."

This was how Banfora expanded their kingdom down to Dakota and made the Dakotans their slaves. The Banforan king was so grateful to Mansa Musa that he and his people came with tons of crops and animals.

"We know that you are the richest man in the world, and our gift is nothing compared to the crumbs of food your servants throw away every day, but we have come with a heart full of gratitude, and we want you to accept our offer," the king of Banfora said as they presented the gifts to Mansa Musa.

Mansa Musa smiled and asked for them to give him a single orange. A servant peeled the orange, and Mansa Musa sucked the juice right in front of the people. "I took this orange to prove that your gift is not too small or in- adequate for me. It is accepted, and I appreciate your gesture. Please go back and plant these crops to make next year's harvest more bountiful. I do not render help so that I can collect what you have. I render help because that is what Allah has commanded us to do. We do not know what tomorrow will bring, so we must fight to make the best of today. When you get the chance to save me tomorrow, you won't hesitate because I helped you when I had the means," Mansa Musa said.

The king of Banfora was still not content. He felt he needed to do something to prove that he was grateful, so he brought out a letter he had written. He had always known that Mansa Musa wouldn't take anything from him, so he had made an alternative plan. In the letter, the king swore always to be loyal to the throne of the great Mansa, to be at his beck and call, and that even after they were gone, the throne of Mali would still have the right to demand one favor from the people of Banfora.

Mansa Musa had never before met a man like that, a man who was obsessively grateful and was ready to go the extra mile just to prove it. He knew that he wouldn't need any favors from Banfora, but not to prolong the issue, he agreed. The two kings signed the agreement, and each kingdom held their own copy of the document. Banfora and Mali lived in harmony for many years, and until his death, Mansa Musa didn't request any favors from Banfora.

Many decades later, long after Mansa Musa and the Banforan king had died, when Mali didn't have as many active gold mines as it used to, a small goldmine was discovered in Banfora. When the news got to the king of Mali at that time, Mansa Sheik II, he grew jealous.

"How could a desolate place like Banfora have gold now when my empire has little to no gold?" Mansa Sheik II demanded.

It irked him to imagine that the throne of Banfora might someday become rich enough to contend with him. He would never let that happen. Mansa Sheik II dug into the archives and found the agreement between Banfora and the throne of Mali.

"They still owe me one favor!" He laughed loudly and wrote a letter to the king of Banfora at that time, King Abu. He reminded him of their agreement and said that Mali was now ready to ask for the favor. He asked for the land on which the gold mine was found.

King Abu was infuriated. He swore that he would never give that land away, no matter what happened. Although he feared that Mansa Sheik II might unleash his army on Banfora and rewrite the history they wrote a long time ago, he still stood his ground and asked Mansa to please request another favor, as the one he asked for was impossible.

Mansa Sheik was in no mood for war. He reported King Abu to the League of Kings, an umbrella union for all of the kings who ruled Africa at that time. They examined the documents and asked King Abu to fulfill his part of the agreement, but King Abu paid them no heed and kept his most treasured possession. Only when the Malian soldiers attacked Banfora and proved to the Banforans that the hands that had built them up in the day could also cut them down at night did King Abu surrender the land to Mansa Sheik II. Ever since, even as kings came and went, generations passed, and the last bar of gold was mined, the enmity between the throne of Mali and the people of Banfora remained as fresh as the leaf of a fluted pumpkin basking in the early morning sun.

* * *

The boat slowed as it neared the riverbank in Banfora. Once safely docked, the sailor extended his hand toward Menkiti. "We have reached Banfora. My money."

Menkiti started feeling up his pocket like he was looking for money. "Um, I put it here. I put—" he stammered as he emptied one pocket after the other.

"My friend, pay me my 1,000 CFA!" the man snapped impatiently.

"I had my money here in my pocket," Menkiti lied, "but I can't find it."

"Ahh! You want trouble this morning?" The sailor stepped closer to Menkiti and grabbed him by the neck of his clothing. "I told you the price before we started the journey, and you said you would pay. Pay me now unless you want the whole of Banfora to gather here and watch me disgrace you."

"Hey, man, calm down. You're shouting," Menkiti pleaded. "How about I pay you with something bigger than 1,000 CFA?"

The sailor stared at Menkiti, measuring him from the tip of his worn-out caftan to the loosely tied turban on his head. "You will pay me with something bigger than 1,000? As poor as you look? My friend, pay this money now or I will call the police."

Menkiti quickly removed the golden necklace from his neck and showed it to the sailor. When the sailor saw the necklace, he loosened his grip on Menkiti, his eyes lit up, and he reached out to touch the necklace, but Menkiti withdrew it from his reach.

"That's real gold," the sailor blurted.

"Yes, it is. And I'm ready to give it to you for a small price."

"How much?" the sailor asked excitedly.

"How much do you have?"

"I don't have much money here. But I can rush home and get you some money."

Menkiti thought about it for a moment. He didn't want to take chances. "You mean you can't give me a reasonable amount of money right now?"

"I have some money from yesterday's business. Today is just starting. I've not made much."

"How much money do you have?" Menkiti asked, and the man opened a small box he kept below his steering wheel. He poured the contents of the box onto the floor of the boat. Then he gathered up the money and handed it to Menkiti. "It's 4,340 CFA, please sell it to me."

Menkiti collected the money and gave the sailor the necklace. Then he and the boys exited the boat and walked into enemy territory while the excited sailor ogled his new luxury, a piece that could buy twenty newer models of his speedboat.

Watching intently as the drama unfolded between Menkiti and the sailor was a young man in an old canoe tucked among the reeds along the riverbank. He drew out his phone and typed a text message: "They are in Banfora."

A few seconds later, he received a reply: "Follow them."

Chapter Eight

As they walked through the busy riverside toward the crowded market, Menkiti's eyes scanned constantly, flashing on everything around them. Although they were in a strange territory where no one knew them, he wasn't going to take any chances. He had no idea what Abdulsalaam was capable of. He very well could have men here as well.

The market was large and overcrowded. The sounds of the traders filled the air—shouting, ringing bells, and singing songs with the name of their wares, all to attract the attention of buyers already overwhelmed with the variety of goods they had to choose from. Many of the traders didn't have stalls. They displayed their goods—second-hand clothes and shoes, groceries, locally made beaded ornaments, and farm produce—under large umbrellas stuck into long pipes and held in place by heavy stones.

Menkiti walked in the middle, with one boy on either side of him. From the corner of his eye, he watched keenly a figure that seemed to be trailing them.

"Hey, can you both hear me?" Menkiti asked in a loud whisper.

"Yes," the boys answered.

"Someone might be following us. We have to be careful."

"How do you know? Did you see anyone?" Hamza panicked, looking behind him.

"Don't look back!" Menkiti snapped. "I didn't see anyone, but let's just be careful. Just follow me wherever I go now, and don't linger. Okay?"

The boys nodded. Menkiti took a left turn between two umbrellas, and the boys followed. So too did their stalker. Menkiti proceeded forward, then took another left turn onto a path that led between two two-story plazas. The stalker walked faster to keep up with them, but by the time he got to the plazas, they had slipped out of his sight.

On the first floor of one of the plazas, behind some bags of beans heaped close to the door of a grocery store, Menkiti and the boys took off their disguises and walked down the last staircase on the east wing of the building. Pacing back and forth by the roadside, Menkiti and the boys waved at several taxis until an empty one stopped and they boarded. All through the ride, Menkiti kept looking behind to see if someone was following them.

Menkiti directed the cab to the house of an old man called Mallam Hayatu. He was Menkiti's great-uncle, the younger brother of Menkiti's late grandmother. It had been many years since they had last seen each other. The marriage of Menkiti's parents had faced much disapproval from both families. Because of the long history of enmity between Banfora and Mali, it had become taboo for people from the enemy territories to marry each other. Despite the disapproval of her family, Menkiti's mother insisted that she must marry the man she loved. The family tried everything they could to make her change her mind, but when she fell pregnant, they realized that there was no use flogging a dead horse. With much pain in their hearts, they let her go, consoling themselves like people who had lost a child. As if in validation of their fears, Menkiti's mother did not live long. She died during childbirth and left her husband to raise their son alone.

Mallam Hayatu was sitting on the porch in front of his house when Menkiti and the boys arrived.

"*Salaam alaikum,* Uncle," Menkiti greeted Mallam Hayatu.

"*Alaikum salaam,*" the old man replied hesitantly, surveying Menkiti's face, looking for any sign of recognition.

"It's me, Uncle. Menkiti, Habiba's grandson."

"Eh, eh, eh!" the old man screamed, and heaved up from his seat to embrace Menkiti. Menkiti was surprised at how strong and healthy the man looked.

"Menkiti, ah, you're a grown man now! Oh, death! Death! You took my sister's daughter away at a very young age. You couldn't even let her see her son grow into a man!" he cried.

"Uncle, it's okay. I'm sure she's in a better place."

"Are these your sons?" he asked, looking at Musa and Hamza.

"*Salaam alaikum*," the boys greeted in unison.

Menkiti looked at the boys. He hadn't prepared for this question, but he was in his early forties, and if he had gotten married on time, he could have boys as grown as Musa and Hamza. "Yes, they are."

The old man hugged them both, explained that he was their great-grandmother's only brother, and chastised Menkiti for not telling the children their family history when he saw the weird look on the boys' faces as he told them about their family tree.

"Halima! Halima! Aminu!" the old man called on his grandchildren. "Where are those children!"

"Baba, I'm coming!" a female voice answered from the backyard. Halima, a beautiful teenage girl wearing a blue hijab came out to meet them. She had an oval face, midnight-black skin, and shiny almond eyes, which she quickly cast to the ground when she saw the teenage boys. Musa's eyes opened wide in admiration, and for a moment, it seemed like the world around him stopped moving.

"*Salaam alaikum*," Halima greeted them, slightly bending on one knee—a sign of respect according to the custom of Banfora.

Hamza tapped him slightly and Musa swallowed hard and look of embarrassment flushed his face. Halima led them into a small room inside the house where they could rest. The boys, both physically and emotionally exhausted, lay down on a mattress on the floor and fell asleep almost immediately.

Menkiti told Mallam Hayatu that he and his sons were traveling to Niger, but he needed to meet some people in Banfora before traveling. While the boys slept, Menkiti went into town to search for somewhere he could sell the gold bars. He asked around and was directed to the few goldsmiths who were still in the business, but none of the ones he visited could afford the bars.

After scouring Banfora all day, Menkiti was exhausted. He made little progress apart from the last goldsmith, who asked him to return in two days, so he could gather enough money to pay for the precious gold.

When Menkiti returned to Mallam Hayatu's house in the evening, he could see that the old man was unhappy. After they had all had dinner and everyone was set for bed, the old man asked to speak with Menkiti in private.

"Those are not your children!" the old man said in a calm, firm voice, looking directly into Menkiti's eyes.

"Baba, I, I..." Menkiti stammered. He peered around the veranda, which led to the other rooms, to be sure that no one was eavesdropping on their conversation.

"Don't lie to me! Who are they? I saw the tattoo on the younger boy's chest when he went to take his bath. That is the royal tattoo of the house of Mansa Musa. Am I wrong?"

Menkiti heaved a sigh, affirming the old man's suspicion. He blamed himself for not warning the kids to conceal their tattoos.

"They are the king's sons, Baba."

"*Allah la illah ila allah!*" The old man put a hand over his mouth. "The news around town is that the king and his family were murdered. Who could have done such a thing? And how did you rescue them?"

"I work in the palace. It was the king's brother that did it."

"May Allah forbid! Please don't say that."

"It's the truth, Baba. I saw everything with my own two eyes. He stormed the palace with hit men and began shooting wildly. Those kids watched their uncle kill their parents. They were lucky I was able to climb through the roof and make it to their room before the assassins. That was the only way we were able to escape."

The old man grieved. "How could a man kill his own brother? For what reason exactly? How could life be so cruel?"

He asked Menkiti what his plan was. Menkiti said that he was looking for a way to get them to the Mediterranean, to Libya or Morocco, so they could try to cross over to Europe.

"Isn't that a long haul?" the old man asked. "Why go through the sea when they can fly?"

"We can't risk that. We don't have any cash, and even if we did, the boys can't go to the bank, immigration, or anywhere public with their real identities just yet. The news of the king's death is already spreading, so the press will be everywhere looking for some news. It'll compromise their safety. We don't know who's a friend now and who's a foe."

Menkiti told Mallam about the hit men who were looking for them at Asante, about the stalker at the market, and that, for all he knew, Abdulsalaam may have some spies watching them right there in Banfora.

"This is really dangerous, Menkiti," the old man said. "If my kinsmen find out I'm hiding those children in my house, they will report me to our king, and I'll be in great trouble. If anyone at all knows they're here, the king could pay to get them and hurt them."

"You see? That's why I didn't tell you the truth in the beginning. I don't want you to live with that guilt. I just need to sell the gold bars I have, so we have some money to travel with. I believe it's my destiny to save these boys. Uncle, please help me keep this secret," Menkiti pleaded.

Suddenly, they heard the door creak. "Did you hear that?" Menkiti asked anxiously. "Someone just touched that door."

"Who's there?" the old man asked, his voice slightly raised.

The sound stopped.

"I said, 'who is there?'" Mallam shouted again. As he grabbed the armrest of his chair, ready to heave himself up and check where the sound was coming from, Halima snuck out from behind the door of the veranda, her face cast to the ground. They watched as a hand tried to pull her back, but she quickly slapped it away.

"Halima! Who is there with you?" the old man asked angrily.

Halima turned back and called her brother Aminu, and he came out of hiding, seemingly as ashamed of their action as his sister.

"You've been listening in on our conversation? Halima, when did you start behaving like that?"

"I am sorry, Baba," she said.

"Aminu! You made her do this. What's your reason for eavesdropping? Do you think we are talking about money, so you can look for a way to steal it?"

"*Haba*, Baba," Aminu protested, his voice mild. "I am sorry. We saw the tattoos when they went to bathe. We were just curious, but we couldn't ask them. I am sorry."

Menkiti felt frustrated. "Have you told anybody about this?" Menkiti asked. He could feel his heart pounding in his chest.

"No, we haven't," Halima and Aminu said in unison.

"Did anyone from outside come here today? Could it be that someone else might have seen it?"

Aminu and Halima thought for a while. "No," said Aminu. "We were the only ones here with Baba. We didn't have any visitors today." He turned to his sister, looking for her to confirm what he said, but she didn't say a word. She simply nodded.

"Listen," the old man began, "you must not disclose this to anybody. Keep this to yourself because if you say anything, we will all be in trouble. If it gets to the king, he will banish us, and he will surely hurt those innocent boys. Do you understand?"

They both nodded. Menkiti surveyed the face of the two teenagers. Aminu's face was still cast to the ground, while Halima's eyes darted around the room, unable to hold the gaze of her grandfather or Menkiti. The remorseful look on Aminu's face gave Menkiti a fresh surge of hope. He was sure that the boy wouldn't say a word to anyone, but could he say the same thing about the girl? What if she decided to gossip to her friends? What if she still didn't understand how dangerous it would be to let this secret out?

"Halima, promise me you won't tell anybody," Menkiti pleaded.

"Uncle, I promise. I won't say a word."

Menkiti wished he could believe her words. The only thing he could do was find a way to move the boys out of this place quickly.

* * *

In the morning, Menkiti found Mallam Hayatu on the small porch in the middle of the compound. A bottle of local rum sat on a stool beside his reclining raffia seat.

"Good morning, Baba," Menkiti greeted him. He then sat on a low bench beside the old man.

Mallam Hayatu gulped down the last drop of rum in his shot glass and spat out the debris of herbs and root inside the drink, his face knotted into a frown like he was being forced to drink it.

"Did you sleep well?" the old man asked after he had gotten over the bitter hot tang in his throat.

"Yes, I did."

"What about the boys?"

"They did too. Thank you."

The old man began to tell Menkiti about a wealthy goldsmith in the neighboring village, Kamolu. He believed the goldsmith would be able to pay for Menkiti's gold bars. As he tried to explain to Menkiti where the man lived, they were interrupted by Halima running into the compound.

"Baba! Baba!" she cried.

Menkiti and the old man rose. "What is the matter, Halima?"

"It's Aminu... Aminu..." She was panting. She bent down and rested both hands on her knees as she struggled to catch her breath and speak at the same time.

"What happened to Aminu?" the old man asked impatiently.

"He has gone to tell the king. I suspected he would go to the palace to sell the information, so I followed him closely this morning when he said he was going for morning training at the football field. I saw him walk into the king's palace!"

"Oh God!" the old man cried. "This boy wants to kill me! Hurry! Quick! You must leave now!"

As Menkiti rushed inside the house to get the boys, Mallam Hayatu ran into his bedroom and took off his trousers. He dipped his hand into the pocket of his inner shorts and brought out a bundle of money. Then he put his trousers back on and went outside.

"Where do we go from here?" Menkiti asked, trembling.

"Here, take this." The old man handed him some crumpled bills and the key to a car parked in his old garage. "Can you drive?"

"Yes, yes, I can," Menkiti stammered.

"Take that car! Hurry now to the bus terminal. Halima will go with you. When you get there, take a bus to Ouagadougou. From Ouagadougou, you can get a bus to Tangier, Morocco. Hurry!"

Menkiti, the boys, and Halima hurried into the car. He tried the key a few times before the engine rattled and then turned over.

"Halima, call my driver and tell him where to pick you up after they have left the park. Okay?" The old man yelled as Menkiti drove the car out of the compound.

Five minutes later, Mallam Hayatu was dressed in his best attire and standing in front of his house when a car drove into the compound. Four armed men got out.

Shadows of Exile

"Mallam, we have information that you're harboring some enemies in your house!" one of the men said.

"My children," Mallam Hayatu started, "how would I have known? I was just on my way to the palace now. I learned that my visitors are princes of Mali. Could you imagine the abomination?"

"So where are they now? Please bring them out!" one of the men said in a commanding tone.

"I sent them away immediately. Such evil beings cannot stay under my roof. In fact, I'm going to the palace to tell the king. We must make sure those people do not sneak into our land again."

The men had their doubts, but Mallam Hayatu was one of the oldest and most respected men in the land, so they couldn't argue with him. Having fooled them, Mallam Hayatu asked to ride with them to the palace, and they let him sit in the front seat while the armed men rode in the back.

Chapter Nine

When they arrived at the bus terminal, Halima took Menkiti and the boys to the loading station reserved for buses bound for Bamako. The place was empty, apart from a few rickety town service buses.

"Let's ask the ticket sellers over there," Halima suggested, and they went to one of the many wooden counters mounted around the loading station.

"We want to buy tickets to Ouagadougou," Halima said to the woman at the counter. She glanced at them briefly, looked the other way, and continued chewing the gum in her mouth.

"Madam, *Ouagadougou*. Bus. We. Want. *Ticket*," Halima said, hitting on each word emphatically and gesticulating with both hands as if she suspected that the woman couldn't understand English.

"It's gone!" the woman said dismissively. She pushed the gum slightly out with her tongue and blew it into a bubble.

Musa's eyes grew wide. He looked around him and then at the woman, just to be sure she could actually see him and his brother. He couldn't believe she had just treated him so condescendingly. No one had ever tried that before.

"You mean there's no other bus? Or another one is coming?" Menkiti asked.

"Come again?" the woman snapped. The quick movement of her mouth caused the bubble to deflate and plaster against her lips. "Bus is finished! Come tomorrow!"

She turned the other way and continued chewing her gum.

"Is this how they talk to people around here?" Musa asked, feeling disgusted as they walked away from the counter. At that moment, it dawned on him how much his life had changed. Overnight he had gone from a royal prince waited on by servants and respected by all to a commoner who a miserable-looking attendant barely had the time for. It felt like he was watching a movie with a poorly written script. He only wished he had a remote he could use to turn it off.

"She's just a garage attendant. They're like that—no manners," Halima tried to explain.

"What do we do now?" Musa asked Menkiti.

"Let's ask other people. That woman is a shrew," Menkiti said. He went to ask a potbellied man checking out the tire of a cargo truck.

"Good morning, sir. Please, do you know if there's any other buses going to Ouagadougou today?"

"No," the man said. "I think the last one just left. They now leave very early because the road is bad. If they leave late, they can't make it to Ouagadougou today."

"So there's no way to get to Ouagadougou?" Menkiti asked.

Musa could tell that Menkiti was frustrated and worried. It was certainly possible that the king's guards could have intimidated Mallam Hayatu into telling them that they had gone to the bus station. It was likely only a matter of time before the police arrived looking for them.

"We are going to Ouagadougou," the man said, "but this is a cargo truck." He pointed at the inscription on the wooden body of the truck written in deep red color: Goods Only.

"Please, sir, you must help us," Menkiti pleaded. "We really need to be in Ouagadougou tonight. It's a matter of life and death."

"Who is dying?" the man asked.

"My wife, their mother," Menkiti blurted, staring at Musa, who was giving him that weird look again. "Please, she wants to see her children before she dies. Please, sir."

The man exhaled. "Okay, I will help you. But the problem is, I am carrying manure in this truck."

"What?" they all exclaimed and took a few steps away from the man and his truck.

"From a poultry farm. For fertilizer," the man explained.

"Oh, is that it?" Menkiti responded, relief audible in his voice. "So, can we go with you?"

"If you want. But there is no space in the front. Just enough for me and my conductor. You and your children will have to sit in the back, on the bags of fertilizer."

"No problem," Menkiti said.

"No way!" Hamza snapped. "There's no way I'm going to sit on that."

Menkiti grabbed Hamza by the hand and drug him away from the truck. "What is wrong with you, Hamza? We're talking about your survival. There's no room to consider luxury."

"Menkiti, we are talking about excrement. About me sitting on a pile of chicken poop. How am I supposed to do that?" He then called for his brother, who came and joined them. "Musa, are you in support of this? Are you really going to sit on a bag of feces?"

"Hamza," Musa said, "we have to do it. Those people may be coming after us now. This place is too dangerous. If I have to sit on it, then so be it."

As they were speaking, the engine of the truck roared to life. They turned and saw that the driver and another young man were already in the cab.

"Are you coming or not?" the driver yelled.

"We are coming!" Musa declared, not letting go of Hamza's hand as they walked to the back of the truck.

Menkiti negotiated for a moment with the driver and then paid him. The conductor—a very dark, short fellow with strong cheekbones and a prominent network of veins under his skin—got down and opened the back of the truck for them. Happily, the bags of poultry excrement occupied barely half of the compartment, while the other half remained empty.

As they climbed into the truck, Halima called out to Musa. He paused and hurried to her.

"Please stay safe," she said, tears forming in her eyes. "I will be praying for you. Okay?"

Musa nodded. He looked deep into her eyes and saw that she was struggling to keep the tears from escaping. A few rolled down her face, and she quickly wiped them off with the back of her hand. Musa drew her in and hugged her tightly. It broke his heart to see her cry. What he wanted was to see her smile the way she had the night before when she had come to give an extra blanket to him and Hamza.

* * *

Musa and Hamza had been sitting on the mattress, talking in low tones when they heard a soft knock on the door. They immediately quieted and instinctively started seeking an escape route.

"Hello, it's me, Halima," a familiar voice said from the other side of the door.

"Oh, give me a moment," Musa responded. He excitedly rose from the mattress without looking at Hamza. Upon opening the door and seeing Halima standing there with the blanket in her outstretched hands, he froze for a moment and stood staring at her. His mouth felt dry, and his heart throbbed anxiously. There was something about her that made him feel spellbound. Maybe it was her almond-shaped eyes and the way she looked into his eyes like a sorceress trying to target his soul; or maybe it was her beautiful smile, and the way her lips moved softly when she said, "I brought you an extra blanket, just in case that one isn't enough for the both of you."

Musa swallowed hard and collected the blanket from her. "Do you want to come in?"

She looked into the room, diverting her gaze as soon as she saw Hamza looking at them. "Umm...not really. But if you're not sleepy, we can sit in the kitchen and talk."

Musa followed her to the kitchen, where they talked and laughed until after midnight when Musa returned to the room and found Hamza already asleep.

* * *

Although leaving her was inevitable, as Musa held Halima, he wished he could ask her to go with them. Musa had not felt an attraction like this since his relationship with his ex-girlfriend, Victoria, had ended. "Bad timing, Musa," a tiny voice in his head chirped. "Bad timing."

As Musa broke the hug, Halima dipped her hand into the pocket of her pinafore dress and brought out a folded paper. "Please call me when you settle in." She squeezed the paper into his hand.

He tried to open it, but she stopped him. "Don't open it yet."

"Why?" he asked.

"You'll make me shy, it's embarrassing," she said, finally giving him that smile.

"Boy, leave the woman alone!" the driver joked.

Musa turned away from Halima and headed back to the truck, ignoring the jibes the driver and his conductor threw at him. What he couldn't ignore as the truck drove out of the lot and they waved goodbye to Halima was that knowing look on Hamza's face, the look he gave Musa each time he showed interest in a girl. Musa had sworn that he was done falling in love so easily, an oath Hamza didn't seem to believe.

"What?" Musa snapped at Hamza.

"Ha-ha, Mr. Lover Boy," Hamza teased, and they both started laughing.

* * *

The truck drove nonstop for about five hours, and then it slowed gradually before the engine creaked and they came to a stop. Menkiti and the boys peered through the spaces between the wooden frames. They seemed to be in the middle of nowhere.

They could hear the driver arguing with some men in French, but they couldn't tell what was going on. Then suddenly the back opened and three men in police uniforms yelled at them to get down.

"*Descendez!*" one of them yelled angrily. "*Passeur de drogue.*"

"*Non, officier,*" the driver argued. "It's not drugs, it's local fertilizer. Fowl manure. No drugs."

The conductor hurried to the back of the truck and brought out one of the bags, opened it a little, and showed the officers.

"*Vous voyez?*" the driver said. "It's fertilizer. Not drugs."

The officer did not give up so easily. He asked the conductor to bring another bag, and then another one, until the tenth bag was opened, and it became obvious that they all had the same content.

"*Vos papiers!*" the officer then ordered as they returned to the front of the truck.

Musa and Hamza leaned against the body of the lorry and watched as the drama unfolded. The driver brought out the documents and gave them to the officer, who began to flip from page to page, reading the words line by line, hoping to find a fault. Disappointment crept up the policeman's face each time he flipped over to the next page. Then he hit on something.

"Aha! Expired insurance," the police officer shouted. He made no attempt to hide his joy at having finally found something.

"My insurance is valid," the driver stated, drawing closer to the policeman to see the date he was pointing at.

"This insurance expired on the 24th, and today is the 27th. You're going to the station." The officer grabbed the driver by the belt. "Arrest them!" he yelled at the other officers.

One of the policemen held Menkiti, while the other tried to grab the conductor, who swiftly slapped the officer's hand away.

"You're struggling with an officer of the law?" the officer who was holding the driver yelled at the conductor.

"This thing expired on Monday. Monday! And you're arresting us?" the conductor protested.

"And so? Don't you know it's a crime to drive around with expired car insurance? This is a public nuisance!" the policeman retorted, frowning at the word *nuisance*, as if to show how serious it was.

The driver continued to argue with the police, which made Menkiti impatient. Menkiti knew that the driver was aware of what the police wanted, and he wondered why he didn't want to give it to them.

"Let's go," the driver said to the officer after much argument.

"What? You want to follow them to the station?" Menkiti asked.

"Yes! Let's go. I don't have money to settle with them."

Menkiti did not like the sound of that. Going to the police station would be a bad idea.

"Officer, how much?" Menkiti asked.

"Two thousand CFA franc!"

"*S'il vous plait, monsieur,* seven hundred," Menkiti pleaded.

They negotiated for a while, until the officers finally agreed to a bribe of one thousand CFA franc. Menkiti gave them the money, and within a few minutes, they were all back inside the truck. This time, however, it was filthy and smelly thanks to all of the bags that had been opened.

By the time they got to Ouagadougou, it was almost nine at night. The boys were hungry and worn out. They'd had nothing to eat all day. Menkiti took them to a road-side canteen at the bus terminal, where they sat on a wooden bench with other passengers and waited for their meal of white rice with a tasteless bowl of sauce. As Musa reluctantly dug his spoon into the food, desperate to fill his groaning stomach, he began to realize how different his life would be. He had gone from eating at the king's table to eating on a crowded wooden bench; from being an heir to a dynasty to being a homeless fugitive. Already this nightmare had dragged on for too long.

Musa looked at his brother, who was gulping down the food. He was glad that Hamza was coping well so far. Right then he made up his mind to quit lamenting the tastelessness of the food and to simply fill his stomach. He needed to get his mind ready for the long journey from Ouagadougou to the Tangier Triangle, the homeland of Moroccan migrant boats.

Chapter Ten

"Hamza, can you hear me? Hamza, wake up! Hamza, please," Musa cried, tapping his brother repeatedly on the cheek. His cheek felt cold, and two trails of dried blood ran across it.

"Somebody help me! Menkiti! Menkiti!" Musa's bloodcurdling scream tore through the dark forest. He lifted Hamza's head and rested it on his legs and continued to tap at his brother's chin. He put a finger under Hamza's nose and exhaled as he felt the warmth of his brother's breath.

"He's alive! He's alive!" he exclaimed, wiping at the stream of blood flowing toward Hamza's eyes from the gash in his forehead. He tore off the sleeve of his shirt and tied it around the wound.

"Somebody help me, please. Help me!" he cried louder, hoping someone would come to their aid.

Musa could hear the sounds of vehicles zooming across the highway, honking loudly as they drove past. It seemed that maybe the worst was over, and the scared drivers were hurrying to get away. He wondered where Menkiti was. The last time he'd seen him was that dreadful moment when they had all fled the bus. Everything had happened so fast. From the moment those four men had walked onto the bus at Ouagadougou, Musa had had a feeling that there was something sinister about them.

There was something particularly odd about their clothing. The men, old as they were—in their sixties—wore baggy trousers, big T-shirts, and baseball caps. If they had spoken with some kind of British or American accent, Musa may have let it pass, but when he heard them speaking the thick Dyula language, he knew that something was not right. The men were either trying too hard to impress or hiding under a disguise.

All of his life, Musa had been taught to question things he didn't understand, to request an explanation for anything that seemed unusual, and not to let go until his curiosity was fully fed, but how could he do that now when he was doing the exact same thing as these men? He too had disguised himself, and he had to be careful of anything that could reveal his real identity. Maybe these men also had troubles they were trying to get away from. As the engine of the bus rattled to life, he buckled his seatbelt. He would mind his own business.

For a while, everything seemed fine. The passengers settled in, some dozing off in their seats as the bus passed through the dwindling night traffic in the heart of the city and merged onto the smooth expressway. It was quiet except for the zooming of other cars that overtook the bus and the husky voice of Lucky Dube serenading them from the tiny speakers below the luggage compartments.

As the bus rolled along, Musa's fears and uncertainties grew. *What does the future hold for me and my brother?* he wondered. He was the heir to one of Africa's richest and most powerful dynasties, but here he was, on a crowded bus, wearing dirty clothes, on the run for his life. His thoughts ran far and wide, the only constant was the agony he found himself in, until finally he drifted off to sleep.

After what turned out to be only a few minutes of sleep, Musa was startled by the sound of screaming close to his head.

"Musa! Wake up! Wake up!" he heard Menkiti calling to him, and he snapped his eyes open and looked out the window. Around them, other buses were reversing as fast as they could. He could see a bonfire roaring in the middle of the road ahead of them, and some angry men armed with sticks and long rifles were stopping the buses and harassing the passengers.

Musa's heart missed several beats. He feared that their doom had finally caught up with them. *Could it be that our uncle has somehow sent these men to hunt us even in this place?* he wondered.

"What's happening? Who are they?" Musa asked as the bus stopped.

"I don't know!" Menkiti snapped, putting his head out the window to try to make sense of what was happening. He saw five angry young men approaching their driver.

"Yes! It's this bus!" one of the young men said.

He looked at the plate number of the bus and examined it again, just to be sure he wasn't making a mistake.

"Yes, it's definitely this one," the young man confirmed.

"Open your door!" a tall, huge, bearded man said, hitting the bus with his stick.

"Who are you looking for?" the driver asked. "What's the name? Let me show you the passenger register."

"You want to be smart?" the bearded man asked. He yanked the door open and grabbed the driver by the collar of his shirt.

Menkiti tucked his head back into the bus. The boys were scared to their core. They looked at him helplessly. It dawned on them that this could be the end of the road. Tears rolled down Hamza's face. Musa drew him closer and hugged him. Then he saw something strange.

Unlike the other passengers, who were all peering out through the window, curious to see what was going on outside, the four men Musa had noticed earlier were lying on the floor of the bus, struggling to squeeze themselves under the seats.

The driver cried out as the angry mob yanked him out of the bus and forced themselves in.

"Where are they?" the bearded man shouted and raised the pistol in his hand. The passengers screamed and fell to the floor of the bus, with some people lying on top of others.

"Hassani! Farouk! We know you're here!" the man barked, stepping on the back of a woman lying close to the door. The woman cried out in pain.

"Keep quiet!" the man commanded and stomped on her again with the heel of his shoe, muting her loud screaming into a mere whimper.

From Musa's position squeezed between two seats, he could see the men burying their faces against the bodies of other distressed passengers, trying their best not to blow their cover. Two more men entered the bus and looked around, but it was impossible to identify anyone with the way the passengers were huddled.

"Ogali, are you sure this is the bus?" the bearded man asked.

"Yes," the tall, lanky one who had first checked out the bus said. "This is the plate number they told me. Bluebird bus from Ouagadougou. Fat driver and light-skinned conductor. They said Farouk, Hassani, Chief Odigha, and Sheik Daula boarded it. It's this bus."

"Everybody, get off now!" the bearded man ordered angrily.

"Stay behind me," Menkiti said to the boys as he squeezed into the crowd of passengers queuing to get off the bus.

One after the other, the passengers stepped off the bus and through the gauntlet of men, who carefully inspected each of their faces. Once a passenger was cleared, the men ordered that person to sit on the side of the road.

Shadows of Exile

"Sit down there!" one of the men shouted at a man who tried to walk off into the bushes. He grabbed the man by the shirt and forced him onto ground.

"Where do you think you're going?" the loud voice of the bearded man demanded as he stormed toward them with his pistol pulled out.

"Nowhere, nowhere!" the passenger cried, kneeling down and begging for his life.

"Don't annoy me or I will blow your head off. I am a freedom fighter. Stand in my way, and I will kill you."

"I am sorry, sir. I am sorry," the man pleaded.

The bearded man turned away and went to join his men checking the passengers.

"Come on now. Hurry up!" he ordered. "You better come out before I fish you out, you greedy old men!"

Menkiti stepped off the bus, was cleared, and stood waiting for the boys to be cleared. As Musa was given the okay and Hamza prepared for his turn, the bearded man noticed Menkiti standing behind him.

"What are you waiting for?" he asked angrily.

"For my sons," Menkiti said, pointing at Musa and Hamza, who had just been cleared.

The bearded man looked at him suspiciously as the boys walked toward him. "Did you say they are your boys?" he asked. Menkiti froze for a moment as the man strode over and looked him squarely in the eyes.

"Yes, they are," Menkiti stammered.

The man didn't seem convinced.

"Is he your father?" he asked Hamza. Hamza nodded fearfully. "Come on, tell me the truth, little boy. This man cannot be your father. You don't even look like him."

"He looks like his mother—" Menkiti interjected.

"Shut up!" the man shouted, and lashed Menkiti's cheek with the back of his palm. Menkiti staggered backward and spit out blood. "Who asked you to speak, you bloody idiot?"

As the man hauled insults at Menkiti, one of the others raised an alarm.

"They are trying to escape!" the voice shouted, and the mob ran to the other side of the bus, where one of the men had jumped out the window and was running toward the woods, while a second one tried to squeeze his fat body through the same small opening.

The mob split into several groups. Some chased after the man who had run into the woods, while others grabbed the one forcing himself through the window. With the mob distracted, the other two men jumped out of a different window and ran directly toward the crowd of passengers, who were now scrambling for safety.

Suddenly gunshots rang out as the armed members of the mob began to shoot recklessly at the fleeing crowd. Musa ran as fast as his legs could take him. He looked around for his brother and Menkiti, but he couldn't see them. He wanted to stop and look for them but knew it would be foolish. Instead, he raced into the heart of the forest, his heart pounding in his chest and his eyes practically blind in the pitch darkness of the night.

* * *

"Hamza, please stay with me," Musa cried as he drew his brother's cold body closer and enveloped him in a tender embrace. Musa was too scared and too tired to lift Hamza in his arms and start looking for a way to get to the road. He was scared they might run into the angry mob or, maybe even worse, a wild animal. Musa made up his mind. It was better to stay there and wait, hoping help would come before sunrise.

The chirping sound of insects and the chill of dew on their skin seemed to be the only companions they would have all night. Then, from a distance, Musa saw the flicker of flames coming toward them, growing larger by the moment. He froze. He felt the urge to call for help, but fear got the better of him. What if it was the angry mob? What if they were still looking for the men?

He heard the sounds of dry twigs snapping under the weight of footsteps as the flames came even nearer. Though his eyes roamed around looking for a safer hiding place, he kept completely still.

"I don't think they're here. We've searched the whole place already," a voice said impatiently.

"Musa! Musa!" a familiar voice called. It was Menkiti.

Musa jumped to his feet. "Menkiti, we are over here," he shouted.

Menkiti and two other men carrying sticks with fire burning at the tips ran to him. Menkiti embraced Musa tightly. "I thought I had lost you," he cried. "Where is Hamza?"

Musa pointed at Hamza, where he lay unconscious on the ground.

"What happened to him?" one of the men asked. He was the older of the two strangers. They were both dressed in worn-out trousers and old singlets that seemed to have been on a long journey from white to cream and were now getting close to brown. Looking at the raffia bags hung across their shoulders and their long rifles, Musa guessed they must be hunters.

"I don't know what happened to him," Musa said. "I think he was hit with a stick. We were separated, and I found him here like this."

The older man dropped his bag and rifle, took his flaming stick, and hurried off the way they had come. "I'll be right back," he shouted to them. "Just wait."

He was gone for a few minutes, and when he returned, his hands were full of leaves. He shredded them and squeezed them until a greenish fluid came out. The man then unwrapped the cloth Musa had put around Hamza's head and inspected the wound. It had stopped bleeding, but the cut still gaped. The old man squeezed the leaves again, dropping the fluid on the open wound.

Hamza grunted out in pain, and his eyes flew open. The old man stuffed the leaves into the boy's mouth and held it closed with his hands. Hamza squirmed and wriggled as he tried to open his mouth. Finally, he pushed the man's hand away and spat out the leaves. He was scared to see the strange face in front of him. He tried to get up, but Musa held him back.

"Hamza, Hamza! Don't be afraid, he's only trying to help you."

On seeing his brother, Hamza calmed down. He allowed the old man to squeeze more leaves onto the wound, which Musa then covered with the other sleeve from his shirt. Only then did they allow Hamza to rise, and once they were sure he had no other injuries, they began to make their way out of the forest. As they walked, Hamza told them how two members of the mob had pursued him into the forest. He tried to evade them but stumbled on a root and fell, and they were upon him before he could get up. They kept asking him if Menkiti was really his father and demanded to know whether they had any links with the old men they were looking for. When they realized they weren't going to get any useful information from him, they beat him, hitting him with a stick, and took everything in his pocket, leaving him for wild animals to feast on.

"Did they get the...?" Musa stopped himself before he could finish the question.

Hamza nodded. "Yes, they did."

Back at the main road, Menkiti and the boys tried to wave down a bus. Their own bus had left as soon as the mob set out after the men, the driver eager to get away before they returned. The passengers who were nearby had been quickly rounded up and boarded; Menkiti, however, had chosen to stay back to look for the boys.

Eventually a bus stopped and allowed Menkiti and the boys to squeeze into the back seat. As they rode along, Menkiti told the boys what he had learned from the hunters who had helped him. According to them, the whole Chinguetti community had been looking for those four elders for the past two weeks. Chinguetti was an oil-rich community in the northern part of Sierra Leone. For years, oil companies had taken unimaginable wealth from the land, but the people still lived in shanties and mud houses. There were no jobs. Only foreign expatriates worked at the oil rigs, so the people survived on farming and fishing, while the government collected huge royalties from the companies.

The oil companies polluted the air, land, and water so much that the fish died, the farmlands were drowned with oil, and crops could no longer grow. The villagers grew furious, and they began to attack the oil companies, destroying their pipelines, kidnapping the workers for ransoms, and chasing them away from their community. The government, fearing a loss of their royalties, fought back. They unleashed the army on the villagers, killing them in droves and burning down their houses, but even then, the villagers didn't give up. The survivors hid in the woods and the creeks and fought from there, bombing the oil facilities and crippling the business activities of the oil companies.

When the government saw that they were losing the war, they called for a dialogue with the village and the oil companies, so the villagers sent four elders to negotiate with them: Farouk, Hassani, Chief Odigha, and Sheik Daula. The oil companies offered the villagers huge sums of money as compensation for their losses and pledged to clean up the oil spills, build schools and hospitals for them, and employ their youth, but the elders did not return to the village to give account of the money they had received. Instead they embezzled it and were looking for a way to run off to Morocco, from where they could escape to Europe.

Chapter Eleven

O n the day the refugees from Guinea crossed the Malian border, Musa was sitting at the long mahogany table with his parents and Hamza having a dinner of rice and fresh fish stew. During dinner, Danga—the tall, hefty guard who spoke with a deep baritone Musa wished his voice would someday be like—walked in and whispered something to Audu, the chief guard, who was standing behind the king.

"Can't it wait? His Majesty is having dinner," Audu whispered impatiently.

No one at the table could hear them, but Musa, who was sitting opposite his father on the far end of a table for twelve, was looking directly at them and could read their lips. He was wishing Danga would speak up so he could hear that deep voice again.

"No, we need to do something now or they might push into the inner cities. They're desperate," Danga said.

"Speak up, Danga," the king commanded, as if he had an eye behind him and could also read the movement of their lips.

Danga approached the king and knelt beside him. "Your Majesty, thousands of refugees from Guinea just trooped through our borders. We've tried to push them away, but they said they would rather die here than go back." His hands tightly clutched the sword strapped to his waist, as if it was the sword that gave him the courage to speak.

The king dropped his gold fork and knife and reached for the bowl of water in the center of the table. A steward, dressed in an immaculate white pinafore, held the bowl closer to him, and King Idris dipped his hands to wash them as he spoke.

"Danga, you don't send away your neighbor whose house is flooding when he runs to you for refuge." He paused and shook some water off his hands, then collected the napkin another steward held out to him. "You know why?"

Danga shook his head like a little boy listening to his father read him a bedtime story.

"Because you don't know when the storm will hit your farm and turn all your hard work into a swamp."

The king removed his eating apron and left the dining hall with Danga and the other guards beside him.

Some days later, the queen prepared Musa and Hamza for what she called their first official princely duty. The refugee camp was crowded with thousands of people. Normally, it was a community primary school, but schools were on holiday, so the king had asked his men to keep the refugees there while they built a better camp for them. Women, men, and children were separated into different halls, where they slept on pallets and tiny mattresses laid on the floor at night and heaped in one corner of the room during the day so they could all have a place to sit and eat.

Musa arrived with the queen and Hamza in the royal convoy. The refugees ran out and cheered loudly as the queen and her children were escorted to the assembly ground with hundreds of guards flanking them left, right, front, and back. As they made their way to the end of the assembly ground, where the queen would stand on the small podium meant for the headmaster to address his pupils every morning, the refugees clung to the wire fences around the school.

The people lucky enough to get a space on the wire held on to it. Others struggled to squeeze their way through, with the shortest ones poking their heads into any open space to get a view of the beautiful queen. The little children cried and threw tantrums until their fathers lifted them onto their shoulders so they too could get a clear view.

It was the first time the royals were addressing the refugees. The king had viewed the large crowd at the border and decided on the best place to accommodate them, but he hadn't spoken with any of them. He only gave the border control workers instructions and mounted some security men to guard the camp.

Like everyone in Africa, the refugees had heard a lot about the kingdom of Mali, the great Mansa Musa I, and the current king, Idris, who many claimed was like his ancestor in so many ways. Everyone wanted to see the royal family, and it made Musa feel proud.

The queen spoke calmly, wearing a smile and waving at the cheering refugees. She told them there was hope for them. That they could stay as long as they wanted and that the king would provide jobs for those who were willing to work and live in their country. They brought two trailer trucks fully stocked with food and clothing, and then they checked the school pharmacy and promised to set up a befitting medical facility there for the refugees.

Before then, Musa had hated being in crowds. Given the choice to play with his friends and cousins, he would rather stay in his room, tucked under his blanket, reading history books about the medieval era, or type away on his computer, writing stories that he would give to his teacher the next day. He delighted in his own company, but Hamza would always drag him out to play, and when Musa wouldn't budge, Hamza would bring his chessboard to Musa's room and wouldn't leave him alone until he gave in and played with him. But after the event at the refugee camp, Musa began to take joy in being in a crowd, especially when the purpose was to help people in need.

***

Now, however, six years later, squeezed among thousands of other migrants who had come to Tangier looking for a way to cross over to Europe, Musa no longer felt that same joy. Here there was no crowd looking up to him with respect and honor. This time he was just one of a thousand other stranded migrants who desperately needed help—help that may never come, even if they laid down their lives in search of it.

Chapter Twelve

The guards at the door bowed as Abdulsalaam walked down the hallway, his burgundy robe flowing behind him, the edges sweeping across the glossy marble tiles of the palace. The door slid open, and he entered.

"How is she responding?"

His voice echoed in the almost empty room, which held only a large wooden bed on which the limp body of the queen lay with a bandage wrapped around her forehead. Several tubes ran from her chest to a beeping cardiac monitor mounted by the bed.

"Not too bad. The bullet almost hit the wrong nerve, but we can handle this," Doctor Kazeem said as he emptied the contents of the syringe he was holding into an IV hanging beside the bed.

A nurse in an immaculate white uniform stood beside the bed holding a stainless-steel tray. The doctor dropped the syringe on the tray and took off his gloves.

"Are you sure you can handle this?" Abdulsalaam asked the doctor as he approached the bed.

He didn't trust Malian doctors, and although the royal house had built many hospitals around the country, the royals never went there for medical treatments. The people of Mali knew this but were not bothered by it. They believed it was only wise for royalty to get their medical care abroad because their enemies could use the health workers against them. The royals, however, preferred to go to Europe because it was no secret that European countries had the best healthcare systems in the world.

Looking at the queen lying almost lifeless on that bed, Abdulsalaam hated himself for hurting her. It had not been his plan to raise a finger against her. All he had wanted was to eliminate King Idris and his sons so he could have her rule the kingdom with him forever. He had known, even as he made his plans, that it would be almost impossible to make her see that everything he had done was for her own good, but whenever that thought came to his mind, he quickly quieted it. Instead, he told himself, "We will cross that bridge when we get there."

* * *

Abdulsalaam had met Farida in school many years ago, while working on a project for a history class in which they were to develop an alternative history built upon the concept of "routes not followed." They were required to outline every major event that had played a role in shaping the history of their country, critically analyze them, and suggest alternative practical measures that would have caused their country to fare better. The students were split into groups according to their continents and then into subgroups according to their countries if there were two or more individuals from the same country. It was in the African group that Abdulsalaam met Farida. She too was from Mali, so they became project partners.

Farida was everything Abdulsalaam wanted in a woman. She was light-skinned and thin but had wonderful curves and voluptuously rounded buttocks that nearly sent Abdulsalaam over the edge each time she wore a tight-fitting dress. During the times they spent together studying in the library, taking notes in class, or digging through the archives at the Gallery of African Arts, Abdulsalaam spent more time admiring how beautiful and intelligent she was than he did focusing on their primary assignment.

One rainy night, after a long day at the library, Abdulsalaam went to drop Farida off at her hostel. As they drove along the slippery roads, listening to Madonna's "La Isla Bonita" with Farida singing along and dancing in the seat, Abdulsalaam pondered whether this was the right time to let her know how he felt. Could it be that she also felt the same way but was waiting for him to make the first move, or could it be that she didn't like him that way? He didn't know if she had a boyfriend. He wondered if she'd be willing to give him a chance. So many thoughts ran through his mind that he arrived at the gate of her hostel before he could clear his head and let the words flow.

"Thank you very much," Farida said as she began to pull off the jacket Abdulsalaam had given her when her chiffon blouse had proved too thin to keep her warm.

"Come on, you can keep it. Or maybe give it back to me later," he said.

She smiled. "I'll be fine. I am home already. I'll just sip a cup of tea and tuck myself into bed." She took off the jacket and placed it on her lap. "So you'll be at Efia's party on Sunday night, yeah?"

"Sure. Should I come and pick you up?"

"No, I'll be going early. She wants me to help her get ready."

An awkward silence hung in the air for a moment as Abdulsalaam struggled to decide whether he should say the words in his mind or wait until Sunday night. Before he had made up his mind, Farida opened the door, said goodnight, and ran into her hostel as fast as she could to avoid getting drenched in the rain.

As Abdulsalaam drove back home, he convinced himself that Sunday night would be the perfect time to ask her to be his girlfriend. He would wait until everyone was immersed in the groove of the party, and then he would take her to a quiet corner by the pool and pour his heart out.

That Sunday, as the party peaked and everyone started getting crazy on the dance floor, Abdulsalaam felt ready to put his plan into motion. He looked all over for Farida, finally finding her by the pool. She was standing with another man who was holding her hand. He felt his heart sink several feet below his stomach. He held on to a light pole for support, his body suddenly too heavy for his legs to bear. He tarried for a while, looking closer at the man holding onto the lady his heart most desired. It was his brother Idris.

Abdulsalaam later learned that Idris and Farida met that night for the first time. They had felt an instant attraction for each other, and Idris didn't want to leave their romance up to chance, and pursued Farida aggressively. From that day forward, Abdulsalaam lived a life of pretense—pretending to be okay with being just friends with Farida and feigning happiness with the relationship between the couple, which later brewed into a royal marriage. Now the days of pretense were over. His brother had taken what Abdulsalaam felt rightfully belonged to him, and all he wanted now was to keep her alive so they could enjoy his reign together.

* * *

"Look, I can get doctors from abroad to handle this, and you'll still get paid in full," Abdulsalaam said to the doctor.

The doctor stared at him briefly but averted his gaze when their eyes met. He seemed irritated with Abdulsalaam's lack of faith in him, but Abdulsalaam didn't care. He knew that African doctors didn't like to be questioned or doubted, especially by the paranoid relatives of their patients. They loved to feel like gods, thrilled at the moment when they walked into the waiting room and relatives of the patients clustered around them asking to know the fate of their loved ones.

"Doctor, will she make it? Why is her temperature still so high? The drugs do not seem to be working. Must she do the surgery? Is there nothing else we can do?" Anxious family members would ask question after question, eager for any words of hope. But these doctors would answer their questions with vague responses like, "We're doing our best. We only treat; God heals."

Abdulsalaam wasn't going to take any such fluff from him. He insisted that the doctor tell him in black and white what the stakes were.

"I said I can handle it," the doctor started. "This is something we do every other day. It's only taking so much time because you didn't put your bullet in the right spot. You were supposed to shoot in-between the sphenoid and temporal, so the bullet would easily pass out of her head before the squamous suture and not hit the brain." He pointed at different parts of his head as he spoke. "But you hit the frontal bone and bruised her left hemisphere, and her thalamus felt much of the pressure."

Abdulsalaam's frown narrowed into a grimace as the doctor spoke. He hated that this doctor was talking as if he if had he shot the queen with the intent of killing her.

"But you don't have to worry," the doctor continued, giving Abdulsalaam a crooked smile. "I have administered some propofol and antibiotics to stabilize her while I prepare her for surgery."

As the doctor blabbed away, Abdulsalaam slipped his hand into his dressing robe and pulled out a gun strapped to his belt. He pointed the gun at Dr. Kazeem, who raised both hands in utter shock, but before he could plead for his life, Abdulsalaam pulled the trigger and pumped three bullets into his brain

"I hope these bullets pierce through both your hemispheres," he spat, and then set the gun on the bedside table without looking at the nurse, who stood frozen by the wall, tears flowing from the corners of her tightly shut eyes, quietly mumbling what seemed like a prayer.

The door opened and three soldiers rushed in, carrying automatic rifles and machine guns. They were ready to shoot on sight if the boss was under attack, but when they saw that Abdulsalaam was sitting beside the bed while the doctor lay on the ground, his blood pooling around him and trickling toward the door, they lowered their weapons and waited for the command.

"Clean that mess," Abdulsalaam said dismissively, picking up his gun and walking out of the room.

He would fly in some Indian doctors to perform surgery on the queen and treat her until she recovered from her wounds and came out of her coma. It was too risky to fly her abroad because she might escape once she regained consciousness and learned what had happened.

He scoffed at the idea of the queen fighting back. Who would she be fighting for? Even if she found a way to end his reign, she would not be able to sit on the royal throne of Mali. She wouldn't have any reason to fight because she had no one to fight for. After all, Nkrumah and the hit men he had sent after Musa and Hamza had returned and assured him that they had killed and buried the boys.

Knowing that he had clipped all her wings, Abdulsalaam couldn't wait for the queen to get well. He would make her warm his bed at night and also give him the papers to all of the properties his brother had acquired that he didn't know about. Apart from the palaces, factories, and hotels the royal family owned in Timbuktu, Bamako, Johannesburg, Tripoli, Lagos, and London, which had been in the family for many generations, he knew his brother had acquired others, and he needed to claim them also. There were cement factories, vast fishing farms, and hundreds of companies all over Africa.

Getting the queen to dance to his music was not going to be an easy task, but Abdulsalaam had his game plan figured out. He would tell her that he had her two sons locked up in a cage and would threaten to feed them to the dogs if she didn't tell him what he needed to know. He would also threaten to storm her village and wipe out every member of her family if she decided to be stubborn.

After he had gotten what he needed, he would then try to win her over. Oh, how he wished she would one day forgive him and be his queen. She was so beautiful and elegant, and each time she walked into the room, even as heads bowed to exhort her majesty, hungry eyes roamed about her body with desires that would never be met. Abdulsalaam was ready to do whatever it took to win her heart and make her see that he did what he did because he wanted to be with her.

"Every woman has a price," he murmured as he walked into his study and picked up the phone on the table. He punched some numbers and then opened the window to get a view of the sun, which was sitting helplessly in the sky as dark clouds clustered around it. Tiny lines of lightning flashed, and thunder roared from a distance away. It was going to be a rainy day, and it was best for Abdulsalaam to make that call now before the network got clogged—the one call that would determine how this whole game would play out.

"Every woman has a price," he repeated, "and I'm ready to pay hers in full." He hoped that the sun—which had turned into a lazy milky ball behind the dark clouds, the droplets of rain, and the roaring thunder—was listening and would be there someday to bear witness that he never set out on a race without running to the finish line.

Chapter Thirteen

A large crowd milled around the entrance of the Tangier Triangle. The people pushed and shoved as they tried to squeeze themselves both toward and away from the seafront. The sounds of festivities filtered through the chattering voices of the crowd as trumpets and drums thundered from the city center where the Tangier Dance Festival was going on.

Struggling through the crowd, Musa could identify three types of people. First, there were the locals, who were clad in flowing white, gray, or cream kaftans with their heads thickly turbaned or adorned with straw hats. Then there were the tourists, who had come from other states and neighboring countries to enjoy the festival. Musa could easily identify them from the enthusiasm in their eyes, the cameras hung across their necks, the way they pointed at the ancient brick houses in the city, and the way they took pictures of everything. Just last year he had been one of them when he had flown in with his classmates from London to experience the festival as part of their African heritage class.

Then there was the third category of people, a category that Musa never would have thought he would be

Shadows of Exile

part of. They were the people who squeezed the hardest through the crowd. They were the migrants, taking advantage of the festivities to push toward the coast without being queried by the police.

Menkiti held tightly to the boys as they moved through the crowd until they finally arrived at a small street where people sold food by the roadside. "Wait here," he said, leaving the boys under an umbrella shed. He walked into a small barber shop and spoke with the shop owner for some minutes before he came out.

"He said the coast is only a few kilometers from here," Menkiti said. They continued walking. It was almost midday, and though Musa and Hamza were famished, food was the last thing on their minds.

When they had arrived in Tangier and found that a huge festival was going on, Menkiti said they had to do everything within their power to get on a boat that day. It was their best chance, as the security agents would be too busy to have time for illegal migrants.

Before their bus was attacked, Menkiti had told them stories of how the police dealt with migrants. He said that sometimes the police disguised themselves and encircled the migrants. Then they would push them into a depression in the ground and heap stones on them. He said that many of the migrants died, while those who survived were thrown into jail. Musa was tempted to ask why Menkiti insisted on taking them through such danger when they could easily move to Ghana, Nigeria, or any other nearby country, but he knew what the answer was. He had come to realize that no part of Africa was safe for them because most African leaders were loyal not to any individual but to whomever sat on the throne of Mali. They all belonged to a cult of sorts that obligated them to do each other's biddings. Almost all of them were so corrupt they could be bought with some juicy number of dollar bills. Musa feared that his uncle could have spies all over Africa.

Menkiti and the boys were lucky to hitch a ride that dropped them off in M'diq-Fnideq, from where they trekked for almost an hour before they got close to the enclave of Ceuta, a Spanish city on the north coast of Africa. For thousands of Africans seeking to cross over illegally to Spain in search of a better life, Ceuta was their only hope. Though a Spanish enclave, Ceuta shared a land border with Morocco and was separated from the Spanish mainland by the Mediterranean Sea. On the land border, there were two mighty steel fences, which migrants had to climb to get into Ceuta.

The streets around the border were crowded with people. They looked like refugee camps. On both sides of the road people were carrying huge luggage, backpacks, and nylon bags. There were women sitting with their children on wrappers spread on the floor eating from plastic bags. Young men and women pooled around a food vendor's shop, eating, laughing, and chatting away like campers who were having the time of their lives. Indeed, it was a good day for them, as the police had not arrested any of them today.

"Let's get something to eat," Menkiti said as they entered the canteen.

While they ate their meal of white rice and lamb-and-pepper soup, they listened to the group on a bench beside them share their stories. One of them said he had crossed over to Ceuta three times, but the police had always found a way to send him back into Tangier. He said he was almost lucky the last time, as he had made it all the way onto a smuggler's ship and they were about to set sail, but the navy attacked the ship and arrested them all.

Another woman told stories of how she had come to Tangier with her boyfriend but left the guy for a boat owner who promised to help her cross over if she became his woman for some time. She said the boat owner went to ferry migrants over one night but never came back. She later heard that his boat had capsized and he wasn't found among the survivors. She had since been looking for her ex-boyfriend, but she wasn't sure if he was still in Morocco or if he had crossed over to Europe. The migrant stories poured in from all corners of the room.

Menkiti looked at Musa's plate and saw that his meal was mostly untouched. "Musa, you're not eating your food?" he asked, concern written all over his face.

"I've lost my appetite," Musa said, dropping his spoon.

"Musa, you need to eat," Menkiti urged. He moved over to Musa's side of the table and held his hand. "Look, Musa, I know you're overwhelmed by all of this, but trust me, we'll get through it."

He looked around to see if any eyes were on them, but everyone else seemed engrossed in their own conversations.

"You see," he continued, "for every single story of failure you hear in this place, there are a hundred others who made it to Europe via this same path. Trust me, I'll do anything it takes to get you over there. But right now, you need to eat. We are going to scale a very big fence, and to do that, you need to be as strong as a horse. Do you understand?"

Musa managed to eat half of his meal before they left the canteen. They trekked down a rough road until they got to the rocky beachfront. It was the Morocco–Ceuta border. Countless migrants clustered around the high chain-linked, barbed-wired fence that separated the rocky beach from the sky-blue Mediterranean Sea.

Looking at those long, scary fences, Musa wondered how he and his brother were supposed to climb over to the other side. They could have gone through the main borders and passed through to Ceuta, but they didn't have their papers. Just like the other hundreds of migrants clustered around the fence, their only chance was to scale the fence and cross over before the police and border agents stormed the area.

There had once only been one fence, but over the years, it had become too easy for the migrants to climb over, so the Spanish government built a second fence behind the first one. Though the fences were made of razor wire that left gory injuries on the hands and legs of whoever tried to climb them, the migrants were not deterred.

Sometimes when the Spanish and Moroccan agents patrolled the border, the migrants would hide in camps they built behind the rocks some distance away from the fence and stay there until the agents retreated. Other times at night, they would gather in the hundreds and storm the fence at the same time; pushing their weight against it so they either overwhelmed the border patrol agents—who would hit them with batons in an attempt to ward them back—or put so much strain on the fence that they created a tear through which a person or two could squeeze themselves through to the other side. Because of this, the Spanish government doubled and reinforced the fence and mounted infrared cameras to detect movement around it.

Menkiti and the boys sat on a rock and watched as people climbed the fence. Some migrants at one side of the fence who weren't using ropes held on to the razor fence with both hands; then they put in their legs and started climbing. Musa's gaze was focused on a group of four men and two women. They cried and grunted as the sharp blades of the fence tore deep into their skin, and he could see bloody rivulets dripping down their elbows. One of the women cried out loudly and jumped down from the fence.

"I can't do it," she cried as her hands shook from the pain of the deep cuts on her blood-soaked palms.

"Metilda, you can do this! Give me your hand," one of the men said, and stretched out his hand for her. She shook her head and went to a small rock where she sat down and began to wipe the blood on the hem of her gown.

"Damn!" the man cursed. He jumped down from the fence angrily and went to meet her on the rock, wearing the frustrated look of a man who regretted embarking on such a journey with a weak person who would always slow him down.

On the other side, people waited for ropes to drop. They took turns holding on to the ropes and climbing over the first fence to the second one, which they climbed using a ladder.

"Go, go, go!" the red-haired man collecting money from the migrants shouted as the ropes dropped from the top of the fence. As one person held onto the rope and started their climb, others squeezed cash into the man's hand and waited for another rope to drop. The man was not alone. There were three others working with him on that side of the fence, but it looked like he was in charge because he was the one collecting the money and stuffing it into the many pockets of his old khaki trousers.

Menkiti went to speak with the man.

"Can I ask you a question?" he asked the man.

"Money, bring money, you cross. Police are coming soon," the man answered dismissively with a thick Spanish accent. He didn't bother to look at Menkiti as he spoke. He grabbed some paper notes a woman was giving to him and counted them.

"No change. I don't have change. Go back or forget change," the man snapped at the woman.

He shoved the money back into her hand and started attending to the crowd behind her, each person eager for the man's attention.

"I want to cross, but after we've crossed over there, what's the next step? How dangerous is it?" Menkiti pressed further.

"Don't ask stupid questions. You want to cross, cross! You want to stay, stay!" the man barked, and gave him an angry stare.

The other migrants shouted at him angrily. From the terror in their bloodshot eyes as they screamed at him to let the man concentrate, Menkiti feared that they could attack him at that very moment. He took a few steps away to try and make up his mind. He only wanted to know what to expect. They barely had enough money on them and they still needed to pay for a boat ride that night.

"Is this your first day?" a man asked Menkiti as he walked toward the fence with Musa and Hamza.

"Yes," he replied.

"Wow, you're lucky. The border agents are very busy at both ends of the border because of the festival. Many people will cross over before they get here today."

The man's name was Kwame. He was from Ghana and had been in Tangier for three months looking for a way to cross over to Spain. He had crossed the fences two times before but was caught and sent back to Tangier. He was very sure, however, that today would be different.

"Bring your boys along," he said to Menkiti. "When we cross over, I know a boat owner who'll help ferry us across the sea."

After they had paid, Menkiti, Musa, Hamza, and Kwame waited for their turn to cross over the razor wire. Like the other migrants who still had some cash to spare, they bought plastic shoes and gloves from the locals at the foot of the fence. The plastic shoes had screws underneath them, which the migrants had to hook between the metal chains as they climbed.

"Go! Go! Time is ticking!" the red-haired man shouted as a rope dropped in front of Musa. Musa grabbed the rope, rolled it around his wrists, and put his leg on the razor fence. He looked beside him. Another rope had just dropped, and Menkiti insisted that Hamza, who was developing cold feet, grab the rope and move at the same time with Musa.

"Come on, Hamza, you can do this!" Musa said. "Just see it as mountain climbing, which you love doing."

"Don't be ridiculous, Musa," Hamza replied as he wound the rope around his wrist, "this is not a mountain. We are talking about sharp blades here. Razor blades, not rocks."

Musa tried to encourage him a little more, but the people behind them were getting impatient, so Hamza put his leg on the fence, closed his eyes, and started climbing. They held on tightly to the rope, which was tied to a pole on the other side of the fence and pulled themselves upward with all the energy they could muster.

Menkiti held his breath and said a silent prayer with every single move the boys made. "God, please don't let them fall," he whispered each time either of them paused to catch their breath.

Just as Musa had hoped, as Hamza climbed the fence, he instinctively returned to his school days in London, when he would sneak out with his friends to go mountain climbing and skydiving. Musa, who had always been scared of heights, would shout and threaten to report him to their father, but he never did.

Even when they got to the top of the first fence, the boys didn't look down. There were two men in the middle of the fences. They held on to the ladder while the boys climbed up the second fence, grabbed another rope tied to the top of the fence, and lowered themselves into Ceuta.

"Move! Move! Don't wait here!" the locals on the other side of the fence shouted as the boys touched down. The boys ran and hid behind a truck a few blocks away from the fence, staying there until Menkiti and Kwame crossed over.

"Today is our lucky day," Kwame said with a smile as they walked on the white sandy beach. They had removed the plastic shoes and were now barefoot. Musa closed his eyes for a while and savored the sweet feeling of the cold sand under his feet and the cool breeze blowing against their clothes, which was making Kwame's voice sound like something echoing from a far distance.

They followed the sandy path to a small beachside neighborhood, which Kwame called Fishers Village. The streets were littered with filth, and children were running around playing soccer with rubber balls and makeshift posts made with two bricks on either side. The smell of roasted fish filled the air, and from behind the shanties and huts made of plywood and bamboo, Musa could see clouds of smoke wafting into the skies as the locals prepared smoked fish to sell later at the night market.

"There is a joint around the corner at the end of this road," Kwame said when he saw that the boys were getting tired. "Many fishermen and sailors used to hang out there, but I want us to meet this particular man. I trust him."

Neither Menkiti nor the boys said a word. They just followed him until they got to the front of the joint. It was an open space by the side of the bay, with several bush bars built with wood and a thatched roof. From the joint, one could see the harbor, where many boats and canoes were docked.

Each bar had a small house behind it where the sellers prepared their dishes. It was a place where fishermen and boat owners hung out to meet their customers, mostly people looking for a way to cross over to the Spanish mainland. Musa could see the long fence they had just climbed, and he wondered why they had to go around all that distance when they could easily walk along the beach and get to the same spot.

At the joint, men were seated in groups of two or more, drinking, eating barbequed fish, and smoking Indian hemp. Menkiti paused as he perceived the smell of marijuana. He looked at the group of men sitting on a low bench smoking, and asked Kwame where the man they were going to meet was.

"He should be inside," Kwame said, and urged them to follow him inside the big stall at the end of the open space.

Menkiti walked closer and whispered to him, "Do they also smoke inside there?"

"Yes! You want to smoke?" Kwame replied with a naughty smile.

"No. My boys can't go in there. They can't inhale that."

Kwame paused and looked at Musa and Hamza. That was the most ridiculous thing he had heard in a long time. Through his stay in Tangier, he had seen children of less than ten years smoke weed like adults who had been doing it for years. He scoffed as it dawned on him that Menkiti and his boys did not know that this was a jungle and there was no room for weaklings who couldn't stand an ordinary smoke.

"Ha! You're not serious!" he said. "These boys are grown. They've never seen Indian hemp before?" He pointed at Musa and gave another naughty smile. "This one never smoked before? You sure?"

"Look, don't be ridiculous. Let the boys wait outside while we go meet the man."

Musa and Hamza sat on a fallen tree by the side of a bush bar. There were a few other people sitting there, and from the eager looks on their faces each time anyone walked out from the big stall, Musa could tell that most of them were waiting for the same reason. Kwame took Menkiti into the stall and asked for Papa Waw.

"Papa Waw is sick. He doesn't come out again," a woman clearing the used plates on one of the tables re-plied. Kwame stood there confused for a moment. The woman carried the plate to the back of the counter at the end of the room and came out with a bottle of beer. She sat the beer in front of a gray-bearded white man sitting with two young black men.

The old man smirked and looked at the woman lustfully as she bent over to uncork the bottle with an opener, showing some cleavage. As she turned around to leave, he spanked her butt.

"*Mi amiga*," he said.

The woman smiled and walked away, swinging her hips, knowing that many eyes were glued to her voluptuous backside.

"Madam, please, do you know any other person that can help us? Me and my friend want to cross over," Kwame told the woman over the counter.

She looked at them for a while and pointed at some men sitting at the extreme end of the room. She told them to ask for Bruno.

Bruno, a slim, tall fisherman with a receding hairline, took them to a corner outside the stall. He told them that he charged one hundred euros per person and that his boat would be leaving the coast by eight that night.

Unlike Kwame, Menkiti didn't have the money, but he told Bruno he would be back. As they walked out of the stall, Menkiti wondered how he was going to raise three hundred euros in a few hours. If they didn't make it across tonight, the border agents would be back on patrol, picking up the migrants who had taken advantage of the festivities to scale the fences.

"How well do you know the people in this village?" Menkiti asked.

"Fairly well. I've been here a few times."

"I have something I want to sell. Do you know anyone who can buy gold?" he asked.

"Gold?" Kwame retorted.

Menkiti nodded.

"As in, gold jewelry?" He instinctively looked at Menkiti's neck and wrist, but there were no ornaments on them.

"Raw gold," Menkiti whispered.

"You have raw gold?" Kwame stared at him like he had lost his mind. There was no way this man that had been loitering around with him for hours, jumping border fences, and walking barefoot could have raw gold.

"My friend, stop joking!" he said dismissively, but to his surprise, Menkiti remained serious.

He called Musa to the side and asked him to give him the remaining gold bar in his pocket. Musa handed it over and went back to sit with Hamza and the other migrants. Menkiti looked around to be sure no one was looking at them. Then he brought out the gold bar and showed Kwame.

"Wow!" Kwame exclaimed, and reached out to touch the precious metal, but Menkiti withdrew his hand and put the bar into his pocket.

"We need to sell it and raise some money. Do you know who we can go to?" he asked.

Kwame was still in awe. He couldn't believe his eyes. He was from the Gold Coast of Ghana, and he knew that

that bar alone could fetch them a lot if they got a good buyer. He looked at Menkiti suspiciously and asked how he got the precious bar and why he bothered to take this dangerous route with his boys when he could have sold the bar for some good money, processed the paperwork, and flown them over to Europe.

"I don't have time for these questions," Menkiti snapped. "Will you help me? I will pay your fare if we can sell it before nightfall."

Kwame agreed, and the boys waited at the joint while Menkiti and Kwame went in search of a buyer.

"Do you think this hand is swollen?" Hamza said, stretching both his hands toward Musa.

Musa took Hamza's hands and compared the two. Hamza's left wrist did look a bit fatter than the right. He pressed hard on the wrist, and Hamza grunted in pain and wriggled.

"Hey, take it easy, man! It hurts," Hamza cried.

"Just chill. If I don't massage it now, it might get worse." Musa continued putting on pressure, but Hamza immediately withdrew his hand, casting an angry stare at Musa.

"Sorry, I was just trying to help."

"You said you were going to massage the hand, not break it," Hamza retorted.

A teenage girl who was sitting next to Hamza on the fallen tree was watching them.

"Can I see it?" she said, and the boys turned around to look at her and then at each other. Though the girl had been sitting there all this while, this was the first time they had paid attention to her.

"Can I?" she asked again, flashing a winning smile.

"Sure," Hamza said, and placed his hand on hers. She started massaging it slowly, running her fingers from the back of his palm to just above his wrist.

"Did you roll the ropes around your wrist?" she asked, and Hamza answered in the affirmative.

She said that's what happened. The ropes had wounded a lot of people; so many preferred to scale the fence with hooks instead of ropes. She said her name was Blessing. She was from Nigeria and had been in Tangier for almost four months.

As the boys chatted with their new friend, they heard a noise at the entrance of a small house behind one of the bars. They turned and saw a woman pushing a girl who looked to be no more than fourteen years old into one of the rooms. The angry woman raised her long black hijab and stuffed it to one side; to give the baby strapped on her back some breathing space. Then she grabbed the teenage girl by the arm and pushed her again.

"Saratu! Get back inside there if you don't want me to bury you alive," the woman threatened.

"Mama, I am tired," the little girl cried, wiping the mucus running from her nose with the back of her palm.

"Just one more, Saratu. One more, and he will cross us over tonight." The woman, in a dramatic twist from anger to compassion, ran her hand through the little girl's long, wavy hair and wiped her tears with the edge of her hijab.

Reluctantly, the girl moved toward the door, into the waiting hands of a heavyset man standing at the door-post grinning from cheek to cheek.

"Is this what I think it is?" Hamza asked in astonishment.

"I can't believe this. Is that really her daughter?" Musa asked, not because he was expecting an answer but because he truly couldn't believe what he had just witnessed.

"You really are new here, aren't you?" Blessing asked. She wasn't at all fazed. She had seen worse scenarios, and she seemed surprised that Musa and Hamza were enraged.

"Well, does that matter?" Musa asked.

"I ask because this happens like every day. When a woman is pregnant, too old, or too unattractive to the sailors, they are sometimes forced to offer up their daughters to smugglers just to cross. It's worse in Tripoli because the smugglers here will ferry you over after sleeping with you or your daughter, but in Tripoli they sometimes just push mothers and daughters into the open seas after being done with them."

Musa felt like asking her if she had done something like that before, and why she hadn't crossed over all these months since this horrific act seemed normal to her, but he bridled his tongue because so many eyes were looking at him, making him feel like he was an alien for seeing things differently from them.

He stood and walked toward the harbor, where some young men were loading cartons into the back of a red vessel docked a few feet from the beach. There was a wide strip of pavement at the harbor, built with railings one could hold on to while getting out of the water. Musa leaned over the railings and cast his eyes to the middle of the blue sea where a huge cargo ship was slowly sailing toward the north, the breeze of the sea blowing the star-encircled blue European Union flag on its stern in all directions.

* * *

The sun began to set, and darkness blanketed the skies. Menkiti and Kwame were still not back, and the boys were beginning to get worried. The sailors were leaving the joint one after the other, heading toward the harbor to push their boats into the sea.

Musa and Hamza stood by the side watching as hundreds of migrants trooped out from an old warehouse close to the harbor. Men, women, and children of all ages rushed toward the boats docked at the harbor.

"*Darse prisa, vamonos,*" a man in the middle of one of the boats shouted. "Hurry up, let's go."

The migrants paused at the pavement and showed their paper tickets to two men standing by the dock. Once each person showed their ticket, the men gave them an orange life jacket and pointed them to either of two dingy boats waiting to set sail. The boats looked old and fragile. They were fishing boats meant for only eight to ten persons, but as Musa and Hamza watched, almost one hundred migrants squeezed themselves into each boat.

They pushed and shoved and shouted at each other as each person struggled to get a seat on the floor of the boats. Not everyone could sit down though, so some just stood in-between those that were sitting down, using others' bodies to steady themselves.

The first two boats sailed off, and two others were pushed into the harbor. Musa and Hamza were now worried that they may not get to leave Ceuta that night. They wondered what could have happened to Menkiti and Kwame and why they weren't back yet. They strolled back to the joint and saw Kwame standing near the fallen tree, looking around like he was searching for something.

"Kwame, where have you both been?" Hamza asked.

"Oh, here you are!" Kwame heaved a sigh of relief. He shouted Menkiti's name several times before Menkiti came running out from one of the stalls where he had gone to look for the boys. As they walked toward the harbor, Musa asked if he was able to sell the gold, but Menkiti had bad news. He pulled the bar from his pocket and showed them. He couldn't get a buyer because no one believed it was real gold. They all waited at the harbor and watched as many more migrants piled into the boats.

"What do we do now?" Musa asked, exasperated.

"Just be patient. There will be a way somehow," Kwame said.

It was getting darker, and more migrants were rushing toward the boats. Voices began to rise as the ticket-checkers argued with the migrants.

"I've shown you my ticket! This is my ticket! It's a lie! Thief!" The angry migrants hurled insults at the two men until they became overwhelmed, and then the people shoved past them and walked into the boats without showing their tickets.

The two men moved out of the way. They knew that almost all the migrants had bought tickets, and it was difficult to keep control because so many people had been able to cross the fence that day.

"Let's go, let's go," Kwame said, and they moved into the crowd. Menkiti held the boys with both hands while Kwame walked in front. They squeezed themselves through the crowd, fighting not to lose sight of each other, until they were all seated on a wooden bench inside one of the boats, a mammoth crowd of other migrants pressing their bodies against theirs.

As the engine of the boat came alive and the boat set sail, Musa heaved a sigh of relief. He closed his eyes and said a little prayer. "Dear God, please let this end in praise," he whispered. He wanted to pray some more, to ask God to direct his path and make this nightmare go away, but the loud voices of the jubilant migrants, who were all happy to be getting to the end of the long journey, which most of them had embarked upon many months ago, drowned out his voice.

Musa felt uneasy as greasy bodies rubbed hard against his. It felt strange to have so many people packed in such a place. There were people who smelled like rotten fish, those oozing with the stench of accumulated sweat, and others who had horrible-looking injuries. The gray-bearded man beside him had offensive breath that practically slapped Musa each time he opened his mouth to speak. Musa turned his face away from the man. Another foul odor hit him, and he felt like he was going to throw up. He squeezed himself into a spot where he couldn't smell the offensive odors, but he still felt the weight of several people crammed against his body. He couldn't believe that after many years of traveling in a private jet, he would now find himself jam-packed alongside hundreds of desperate people scrambling to get to Europe, a continent he had always visited with ease. "Oh see how the mighty have fallen," he cried, shaking his head.

He closed his eyes and savored the cool breeze and the smell of the sea wafting into his nose as the boat sped farther and farther into the Mediterranean. His relief, however, was short-lived. He felt the boat take a sharp turn and heard all the passengers onboard scream. He snapped his eyes open and saw a heavy storm raging toward the speeding boat.

Chapter Fourteen

66 Jesus! Jesus!" some of the migrants screamed as the helmsman struggled to steer the boat away from the storm.

Musa could see the storm raging furiously, and he feared that it would swallow the boat in a single gulp. The helmsman held on to the wheel, clenched his teeth, and dragged it toward the right in order to sail back toward the bay, but the billowing waves tumbling under the boat seemed to have a stronger pull on the rudder. The boat tossed from left to right and back to the left again, throwing the migrants around as the water beneath them roiled. The migrants held on to the wooden body of the boat, the edge of the benches, and each other as tightly as they could, but with every toss of the wave, one or more lost their grip and crashed on top of the others.

The tiny voice of a helpless baby cried out as the wave threw the mother and she crashed against the wooden edge of the boat. The woman lay there motionless, with her arm pressed against the head of the baby strapped to her back. The migrants watched as the baby's heart-wrenching cry thinned down to inaudible gasps, but no one could do anything. The waves became stronger, and some of the wood began to pull from its moorings, yielding to the intense pressure of the traumatized people within it.

Musa, who had scrambled his way to Menkiti, held on to the bench and on to Menkiti, who was holding Hamza with his other hand. "Hold on tight!" Menkiti shouted. "No matter what happens, don't lose your grip on the boat! Do you hear me?"

"Yes!" the boys shouted.

Musa's hands were shaking. He could feel his heart pounding in his chest. The sound of cries and prayers became louder. Hot tears formed as he saw his life flash before his eyes. He wished he could turn back the hands of time so he could do things differently. He would insist that they hang around until they find way to sell the gold bar. Or maybe they would totally forget the idea of trying to cross this bloody sea and go to another African country to apply for asylum without fear of betrayal. If only he hadn't run away from Sikasso. He should have run into the barracks and commanded the army, in the name of his father, to storm the palace and take it from the hands of his traitorous uncle. But right now, those were just mere wishes, and as the storm slammed against the boat, throwing the helmsman backward against the screaming migrants, Musa realized he couldn't wish this scary reality away.

As the strong winds battered the boat and set it whirling in circles, the salty water splashed up and poured into the boat. It sprayed Hamza's wounded forehead, and he screamed at the pain. He pulled his hand away from the bench and latched it on to his forehead.

"Hamza! No!" Menkiti screamed as the boy tried to withdraw his other hand. "Don't leave the bench, Hamza. Hold the bench."

As Hamza tearfully let go of his forehead and held tightly on to the bench, the storm raged closer and closer, and in one swift motion, a giant thunderous wave slammed against the center of the boat and split the dingy old vessel into two. Everyone screamed as the impact threw them in different directions into the deep, cold waters of the Mediterranean, which had effortlessly swallowed up tens of thousands of migrants before them. Many yelled and struggled to swim against the waves of the stormy sea, but they were no match for the it.

Musa closed his eyes. He held his breath and scrambled with both hands, hoping to grasp something he could hold on to. He slapped his feet vigorously against the water, swimming tirelessly until he got to the surface. He pushed his head out and started panting for breath.

He looked around and saw people in orange life

jackets tossing around in the sea. He searched for anything that looked like land, maybe an island nearby, but the waters stretched as far as he could see. He wondered how he was going to make it out of this place. His body was freezing, and even though he was still in the water, he could feel the skin on his face drying up.

He saw a dark object floating on top of the water some feet away from him, and he quickly started swimming toward it. The storm was beginning to calm down, but it still pushed the object away from Musa. Although he was scared and tired, he began to stroke faster.

"You can do this, Musa," he murmured, and propelled himself forward until he was able to grab the object. It was a piece of the boat. Musa wrapped his arms tightly around the wood and allowed himself to move as the water willed.

"Hamza! Menkiti!" he yelled as he floated along. But there was no response. The sea was now calm and peaceful, and the storm, which had caused chaos in the blink of an eye, had disappeared into the darkness.

Musa cried and prayed that his brother and Menkiti would come out safe somehow. Just like Musa, Hamza was a good swimmer, but there had never been a time when they'd had to swim to save their lives. They had a large swimming pool in the palace that they hardly used, but each time they went on vacation at any of their family hotels, the boys swam like fishes. When they were much younger, their mother had hired a personal trainer to teach them how to swim. For fun, the boys had often competed to see who could stay under water longer. They'd had no idea then that a day would come when they'd need to use that training to save their lives.

"What if Hamza doesn't make it? What if he dies?" Musa's fears were gradually getting the better of him. He was weak. He couldn't move his hands again to swim in the water. He just held on to the wood, tighter than a terrified child would hold on to his mother. He rested his head on the boat and allowed himself to pass out into sleep, trance, death, or any other realm that life decided to plunge him into. He didn't care what happened next, because nothing made sense anymore.

* * *

"Aqui! Aqui!" a voice shouted in Spanish. "Over here! Over here!"

The voice filtered into Musa's ears, sounding like echoes from far away. The shouting continued, however, and then he heard the sound of a speeding boat coming toward him. He opened his eyes and then shut them immediately as the bright morning sun pierced his eyes.

He opened them again slowly. His vision was blurry, and he could feel the veins in his eyes straining. He wiped his eyes with one hand while holding on to the wood with the other. Two white speedboats were racing toward him.

On the body of the boats, he saw *Armada Espanola* written in bold red paint. Musa knew that it meant Spanish Navy. He breathed a sigh of relief, and for the first time in what felt like a long time, he smiled. He had made it to European soil.

Two men dove in and carried him to the boat. Desperately he looked at the other three migrants sitting on the floor of the boat, trying to catch their breath. None of them was Hamza or Menkiti.

With tears in his eyes, Musa looked at the sailors. "Please, sir, are there other boats? Have they found any other survivors?"

The sailors were in no mood to answer any of his questions. They commanded him to sit down and keep quiet. "You should be happy we didn't shoot you on sight!" one of them said, staring at Musa and the other migrants like they were common thieves who had come to steal what belonged to them.

The boats docked at a seaport, and they all stepped out. Immediately, Musa saw the row of bodies lying by the beachside, many of which had orange life jackets still strapped to their chests.

Musa's heart began to pound. He pulled his hand away from the Red Cross worker who was leading him to one of the red ambulances parked by the beachside and ran to the dead bodies and began to check their faces. There were over fifty of them. He cried bitterly, praying and hoping that his fears wouldn't become reality.

As Musa went from one unfamiliar face to the other, he felt air draining from his lungs. He didn't know what he would do if he found what he was looking for. Then it happened. He saw a body lying on a small rock with both of his hands spread wide. His face was dry and swollen, and his bloodshot eyes were wide open, looking helplessly at Musa.

Musa cried bitterly and shook the body vigorously. "Please wake up, Menkiti. Please wake up!" he shouted, but Menkiti was long gone, dead and motionless.

The Red Cross lady who had been watching him in tears held him by the shoulder and helped him stand up. She walked him away from the dead bodies to the back of the ambulance and put a thick red towel around him. She tried to calm him down, but Musa would not be comforted. His tears flowed endlessly, easing only when he saw another boat dock by the beachside and another group of rescued migrants troop out. From that group Musa saw his brother running toward the dead bodies. Musa screamed Hamza's name, and Hamza's eyes brightened as he saw him. They ran toward each other and glued their bodies together in a fierce embrace.

"Oh, you made it! Hamza, you made it," Musa cried.

Chapter Fifteen

Over the past two weeks, the offshore migrant center had been hit by the worst case of migrant inflow ever. They had rescued over nine hundred migrants from boats, some of which were stuck in the sea and others that had capsized and thrown their passengers into the ocean. About three hundred people did not live to tell the story and were buried in a shallow mass gave off the Strait of Gibraltar.

A large black van drove to the gate of the migrant center at Malaga and stopped for routine checks. A tall, brown-haired man dressed in an army uniform—a rough blend of olive green, coffee brown, and cream—and clutching a machine gun by his side walked to the back of the car where the migrants sat, separated from the driver by strongly reinforced iron bars. The soldier walked along, slowly looking at the migrants through the glass windows. The migrants held his gaze. No one said a word or made any gestures at him, not even when he smiled at a baby playing on her mother's lap on the seat behind Musa and Hamza. Being mostly Africans, the migrants feared the police and every other uniformed person. Some, like Musa, had been threatened by the very people who had rescued them, whereas others had lived under police and army brutality in Africa for so long that they had learned that anyone in uniform had no good intentions toward them. The soldier walked back to the front of the car and waved at the driver to proceed.

The van stopped in front of a long yellow building, and the driver's assistant rushed down and opened the back door. He lowered the gangplank, and the migrants began to alight in hesitant groups of twos and threes. Nine workers in different uniforms—sky blue, maroon, white, and some shades of colors that Hamza was too hungry and worn out to place—queued up to receive them. The first in line, a man dressed in a sky-blue T-shirt wearing a warm smile, shook the hands of each migrant and said with practiced enthusiasm, "You're welcome. Please feel free to talk to us if you have any health concerns." As he spoke, he looked at the face of each migrant and repeated the same words in French each time he felt they didn't understand what he said.

The migrants shook hands with the man briefly and proceeded to collect a bottle of water from the lady next to him. Another worker wearing the same sky-blue shirt handed them food tied up in plastic bags, and as they filed into the building, a middle-aged woman pinned a number tag on their shirts. "Please memorize your number, and always listen for when you'll be called on the public address system," she said.

Musa and Hamza tore the plastic bags open as soon as they sat down in the lounge, which held hundreds of other migrants. Without saying a word to each other, they dug the plastic spoons into the bags of smoky hot jollof rice. Hamza pushed the fried fish tail to the side and munched on the rice dutifully until he was left with only a few scattered grains.

"Give way, give way!" a woman shouted as a wounded man was wheeled by uniformed men into the lounge. Two nurses took over the stretcher in the lounge, moving the wounded man into the next room and closing the door behind them.

"What do we do now?" Hamza asked.

"I really don't know, but I think we should talk to somebody. We can't keep hiding our story forever. We can at least apply for political asylum and see how it goes from there."

"What difference would asylum make? It's either we get help to fight back or Uncle keeps coming for us. Look around. One person among all of these people sitting here looking needy and helpless may be here because of us. They could be watching us and could kill us in our sleep."

Hamza continued to voice his fears. The sea had changed something in him. Trapped in that corrosively salty sea, Hamza had had to bear more pain in nine hours than he had borne all his life. When the waves slammed against their boat and split it into two, he found himself thrown under one side of the shattered boat. The heavy wood pressed him down deep into the water. Hamza struggled to breathe and to lift the heavy load crushing him, but as he put his two hands above him, trying to push the boat away, the boat seemed to tumble to the other side, its hull slowly sliding toward his head. He forcefully swallowed some gulps of water and choked. He tried to cough the water out, but more and more rushed down his throat through his mouth and nostrils. He was drowning. Everything was blacked out in the darkness of the night. His forehead was bleeding, and the salty water bathing his wound sent stinging sensations down his spine.

As he came face-to-face with death, he heard the voice of his father speaking into his ears. *"Hamza, you're a fighter. Hamza, you can't quit."*

His spirit protested that he was tired. Both of his hands fell to his sides, and he couldn't find the will to move them.

"You have the energy, Hamza. You can do this. Swim. Just swim!" the voice persisted. He moved his hands and legs. Stroke after stroke, he swam away from underneath the heavy planks and rose, finally feeling the chilling breeze of the night against his broken forehead.

He touched the wound but couldn't feel anything. His body had become numb, and even when the bright shining halogen light of the Coast Guard's torch flashed in his eyes, he didn't snap his eyes shut. The last thing he remembered was a man jumping into the sea and swimming toward him.

When Musa hugged Hamza earlier that morning, he realized something had changed about him. Hamza didn't flinch when Musa tried to touch his scar, nor did he cry when Musa took him to see Menkiti's swollen body where he was laid with the other corpses. He just stood over the dead body, with two clenched fists pressed against his hips, and shook his head slowly with the patronizing grief of a person feeling empathy for a mourning stranger. He didn't shed a tear or touch the body of the man who had risked everything for them. Musa was sad about this, but he held his tongue. He knew something had changed. This wasn't the little brother he had known before the storm. That Hamza, would have yelled and wept, shaking Menkiti's still body until he was dragged away. Musa was convinced that the storm had taken away his brother's ability to feel pain. He blamed the sea. He blamed fate.

Musa noticed the way Hamza's eyes darted from one corner of the lounge to the other. He knew he was looking for any suspicious eyes that may be staring at them. But no one seemed to be looking at them. Many of the migrants were munching their food and some were engrossed in low-toned conversations with the people sitting next to them. Others paced back-and-forth impatiently as they waited to hear their numbers.

"Hamza, calm down," Musa said, grabbing his hand. Hamza flinched and pulled his hand away.

"Oh, sorry. Is that your wounded wrist?" Musa asked.

Hamza nodded and began to rub his hand gently to soothe the pain away.

Musa remembered Blessing and wondered if she had made it. He thought about her and the other people he met in Ceuta. Did their boats get to Spain in one piece? Did they get into a storm and manage to somehow escape ? Or were they now corpses too, buried in a shallow grave or still floating with the tide somewhere in the Mediterranean? So many questions ran through Musa's mind, questions he would likely never get answers to.

Hamza was still massaging his wrist. His face was tightened into a grimace, and Musa could tell with a glance that the pain was severe. Musa stood up and walked to a man standing at the door leading into the dispensary. He asked if he could get an ice pack to massage his brother's swollen wrist. The man refused to give him an ice pack. Instead, he asked for Hamza's number and went into the other room. Musa stood there contemplating his new reality of having to ask for everything, or worse not getting it.

Later that evening, some officers from the Spanish immigration service came to the center. They entered an office and asked for the new migrants to assemble at the lounge. They all filed out from the large hall where they had been given blankets to find a space and squeeze themselves in because every bed space had already been taken.

Musa heard his number announced over the public address system. He walked into the office where three men and a woman sat at one end of the table. He bowed slightly as his eyes met theirs. The woman asked him to sit.

The woman then surveyed his face, trying to decide what language would be most appropriate to use. "Do you speak English?"

"Yes, I do."

The woman exhaled. "What is your name?"

"I am Musa Bala Idris, ma'am," Musa replied.

"Musa, what are you doing on Spanish soil? Do you know you could have lost your life in that sea?" the woman asked.

"I didn't have a choice," he replied, trying so hard not to let the tears forming under his eyelids drop. "This was the only place we could run to for safety. My brother and I would have died if we didn't make this move. Our uncle—"

One of the men edged toward the woman. She brushed her long blonde hair backward and tilted her ear toward the man.

"Seems like we're about to hear another 'My father is the president of Zimbabwe' story," the man said and laughed. The woman giggled and turned back to Musa, her smile transforming instantly into a frown.

"What do you mean? What are you running from? Did you commit a crime?"

"No. I am the crown prince of Sikasso, the throne of the Mali kingdom—"

"Here we go again," the man cut in with an exasperated look on his face.

Musa ignored him. He continued with his story. He told them of how he had watched his uncle murder his father and how they had escaped from the palace through a hidden tunnel.

"Young man, we've heard this story over and over again," one of the other men interrupted. "Every single one of you seems to be a prince, a fleeing king, or a wanted politician. Can't you at least be creative in your lies and know when one lie has been so overused that it becomes a cliché?"

"You never can tell. These could be magical lines," the woman said, punctuating her sarcasm with a shrug. "After all, Americans still fall for the 'I am a Nigerian prince; my money is stuck in the bank due to next-of-kin issues after the death of my father. I'll be coming to the U.S. to start a new life with you, but I need you to send me some money to help clear issues with the bank, so we can be filthy-rich together' nonsense."

"Madam, I am not telling you lies. Look at this." He pulled his shirt up to his neck and pointed at the royal tattoo on his chest. "This is the tattoo of the royal house of Mali. It is the seal of our forefather, Mansa Musa I. You can check the Internet or any history book. This is my story, not some made-up fable. You can check the news; I am sure you'll read about the slain king of Mali. That is my father," Musa insisted.

Tears were beginning to drip from the side of his eyes, making his throat scratchy as he continued trying to convince the immigration officers. But the officers said they had heard this same story repeatedly and had seen so many fake tattoos that his didn't make an impression.

They told him about the woman who had just left the room before his number was called. The woman was wearing a long dress made of Ghanaian prints, with a hijab wrapped around her face. They told him that she too had claimed that her husband had just been murdered by his political opponents, and she managed to escape with her two children, but the children died during their crossing. They said her tears were more convincing than his.

The officers asked Musa his age, and when he told them he was seventeen, they said he was too young to work, so they'd need to find him a guardian. One of the men wrote his details down on a register and took a picture of him before they sent him out of the room.

"Are they going to deport us?" Hamza muttered when he saw Musa's downcast face.

"I don't know," Musa said, and shook his head. Then he put both palms over his face to keep his tears from rolling down.

"They didn't believe me," he managed to say.

Hamza placed a hand on his brother's lap and said, "I'll try. I'm sure they'll believe us when I give them the exact same account you gave."

Musa hoped Hamza's interview would be more successful, but after Hamza went into that room and came out, it became clear their case was sealed. Hamza narrated that as soon as he got into room and sat down, even before they asked him what his name was, the woman dropped the bombshell.

"Hi, Prince," she greeted him, smiling at him like an excited young girl who just saw a cute baby. "Please take a seat, dear. But before we start, if you intend to tell us that you're a prince or governor's son running away from your father's political enemies, please save the story, because seventy-five others have said it before you."

* * *

New European Union laws prevented the Spanish authorities from deporting the migrants. During the two weeks Musa and his brother stayed in the camp, many more Africans were saved from the sea, and the camp became so crowded that some people had to sleep on the paved floors outside or under the old stationary vehicles parked in the concrete-floored compound.

On the ninth day, they separated the young migrants who were less than eighteen years old and put them in a different hall. One after the other, they started taking them away to place them in foster care. The Spanish government couldn't handle the massive surge of refugees that hit them, so the European Union intervened. They placed an ad for willing guardians abroad to apply to be the foster parents of some of the minors in return for a monthly wage.

On the fourteenth day, the officers came into the camp and called some numbers. Musa's and Hamza's numbers were among those on the list. Some families in the United States had applied to be their foster parents. They gave Musa a nine-month refugee visa and a passport and said his good conduct could get him an extension. He opened it and saw his picture with a strange name written below it: Mandy Patrick. He showed one of the officers the papers and told him they had made a mistake, but the officer laughed and said, "Get used to it. That's your new name."

Chapter Sixteen

Musa's first few weeks in the United States were the most depressing of his life. He could not stop wondering what was happening with Hamza.

The morning they were separated the Spanish authorities had asked them to file out into the yard, bringing what belongings they had as well as their passports with their visas. For over an hour, they waited without anyone coming to address them. Then a blue SUV arrived at the migrant center. A petite blonde woman descended from the blue SUV and walked toward the entrance of the building. She shook hands with the medical workers at the entrance, and they talked for a while before one of the workers went inside and came out with a handheld microphone.

"Listen up, everyone," the man said. "If you hear your number, please go into the SUV parked over there: 7321, 8711, 8156, 1388."

Musa and Hamza turned and looked at each other and at the tag on Hamza's shirt. "Eight-one-five-six, that's you?" Musa asked with quivering lips.

Hamza nodded, stood up, and walked toward the car, as did the other youths whose numbers had been called.

Musa rose and went to speak with the petite lady, who was standing beside the announcer, as the announcer repeated his announcement in French.

"Madam, where are you taking them?" Musa asked to the utter surprise of the lady, who turned around and looked him over from the tangled hair on his head to the bruises on his cracked feet.

"Excuse me?" she asked, surprised at the unwavering boldness in Musa's eyes.

"I said, where are you taking them? That's my younger brother over there." He pointed at Hamza, who was leaning against the car, waiting as the driver adjusted the first row of the back seat to create space for some of the kids to enter the second and third rows.

"We are taking them to the airport," the woman said.

She wasn't the type to respond to questions from illegal immigrants who kept making her job more difficult every day, but there was something about Musa that made her feel she needed to answer him. He did not seem timid like the other immigrants she had met since she had started working this job two years ago.

"Your brother is going to be safe; we are taking him to meet a family that has applied to take care of him. Do you know what *foster care* means?" she asked, looking at Musa condescendingly, trying to gather the simplest words with which to explain it to him.

"I know what foster care is," Musa replied, giving her an angry stare, "but you just can't separate us. We've been together all our lives."

"Oh, poor child," the woman gushed, exchanging a brief glance with the announcer. "Don't worry, your brother will be well taken care of. He's going to have a new family that'll love and care for him, okay? You don't have to worry."

"Madam, you don't understand," Musa cut in, feeling insulted at her patronizing tone. "We need to be together so I can be sure of his safety. It's not safe for us out there, and our chances of survival are better if we stick together."

"What is he talking about?" the woman asked the announcer. The announcer became furious. He grabbed Musa by the waist of his dirty black trousers and pulled him toward him angrily.

"Look, young man, you need to stop these nonsense tales and allow us to do our job. You think we enjoy watching the bunch of you dump yourselves on us every day like houseflies perching on a dead animal?"

Musa slapped the man's hand away and continued talking to the woman. "Ma'am, there are people out there who want to kill us. I can't let you take him out of my sight. He is all I've got. You can take all your privileges and kind gestures away, but please allow us to stick together."

Musa's voice was spiraling upward and drawing attention from all over the yard. The migrants crowded together, watching them from a distance, some of them whispering to the others, trying to figure out the cause of the uproar.

The woman widened her eyes. "Did you not want to leave your country and live in a better place? That's what we are offering."

"We aren't just looking for a good country!" Musa snapped. "We are looking for protection. Do I look to you like someone who's just desperate to live in Europe? Why can't you see that everyone here isn't the same? Why is it so difficult for you to do a little background check and find out who's telling the truth and who's telling a rehearsed lie?"

"Young man, keep quiet!" the announcer ordered.

"Don't you ever try to bark orders at me again!" Musa shouted at the announcer. "How dare you!" He stepped toward the man, looking him squarely in the face. The man cringed in what seemed a mix of fear and surprise.

Musa turned back to the woman. "Madam, you have to believe me. You won't be doing us any good if you separate us. I won't feel at peace knowing that my little brother is out there and may fall into the hands of our enemies."

The woman looked sober, but before she could say a word, two angry-looking men dressed in army uniforms seized Musa. As the men dragged him to a small cell near the security gate, Musa kept his eyes on Hamza, who was crying profusely as the driver's hand gently lowered his head and helped him into the back seat of the SUV.

Clinging tightly to the metal bars of the caged room, Musa watched as the car drove out of the compound. Through the window of the car, the only thing Musa could see was Hamza's head buried in his palms. He didn't even get a chance to say goodbye, and it made his heart break into pieces.

Later that evening, the immigration officers took him into a room and talked to him. Musa just listened but did not say a word. They warned him to stick to his new name and forget whatever he thought happened in his past. They told him if there were people out there who really wanted to kill him, it was best for him to hold on to his new identity so no one could trace him to wherever he was going.

"Don't complicate things for yourself when you get there," they said, and then asked him to leave the room.

Before another car came that evening to take Musa and a few others to the airport, he heard two immigration officers whispering to each other in Spanish. One told the other that Musa was suffering from posttraumatic stress disorder due to the near-death experience he'd had at sea and it was making him delusional.

* * *

There were a lot of things Musa needed to get used to. He needed to get used to being called Mandy Patrick. At the airport in New York, he had walked right past the couple holding a blue placard with the words Mandy Patrick and heart shapes drawn all around it. He had been looking for a sign that said Musa, but when he walked by all the people holding up placards and didn't see his name, he pulled out his passport from the inner pocket of the gray jacket the immigration officers had given him and murmured the name a few times. "Mandy Patrick, Mandy Patrick. Musa, you need to get used to this name," he said, and turned back to check the placards he had already passed.

The excited couple embraced him as he walked up to them. The woman said her name was Maria. She was Latin American and had short blonde hair, hazel eyes, and a smile that showed off a broken upper tooth. Maria told him that they lived in the Bronx, but that her husband, Andrew, was born and raised in Manhattan. Andrew collected the small backpack from Mandy's back and opened the door of an old rickety car for him to enter. They seemed to be really happy to meet Mandy, and it made him feel at ease. Maybe this was really going to be a good opportunity to heal and to be part of a family again.

From the front seat where she sat, Maria kept turning back to look at Mandy, to ask about his first experience on an aircraft or to point at one building or the other and say things like, "You see that? Can you guess how many stories that building is? It is twenty-five stories, and you have to climb it with an elevator. Do you know what an elevator is?"

Mandy would peer through the window and look at the buildings, feigning a surprised face. Then he would shake his head, and before he could mutter the word "no," Maria would be pointing at a public bus with an upper and lower deck. "I am sure you must have seen this in the movies before. This is what some of the buses in America look like. You have the upper deck and the lower one."

"Wow, will I have the chance to ride on one of them?" Mandy asked, pretending to be as excited as they expected him to be. Although he had been in New York a few times and had seen the same kind of buses in London, he had never been on any of them before. He hadn't even imagined ever using public transport, but now, with the life of a commoner lying ahead of him, a tiny part of him looked forward to riding those buses.

"Yes, of course." Maria smiled at him and at her husband, whose eyes were focused on the road as they drove through the early evening traffic. Mandy was tired, and all he wanted to do was have a warm bath and sleep. But Maria kept talking and pointing at different things she thought Mandy had not seen in Africa, and it took all of his willpower not to shut her up and tell her that this was not his first time in New York and that, even if it had been, he had lived a good part of his life traveling to places that she may never reach in all her life.

Although Mandy did not expect to see a shimmering smooth driveway with neatly manicured lawns on both sides and a sparkling spring overflowing with fresh water, like what his family had in Sikasso, his jaw dropped in disappointment when the car drove into a clustered neighborhood with houses separated by spaces barely spacious enough to accommodate two cars. The engine squeaked and the car stopped. The chatty Maria came and opened the door for him, and he came out and they wait for Andrew to go and park the car.

"Here we are!" She spread her hands toward the tall brick building.

Mandy looked up at it. He could guess that it was nothing less than ten stories, but he didn't ask. Mandy just followed them through the door into a stuffy passage and began to climb a flight of stairs. Maria said that the elevator had broken on Thursday night. It was already the weekend, so they didn't expect the landlord to fix it before Monday.

Mandy held on to the metal rails, lifting his tired legs as they climbed toward the fifth floor, which was where Maria said his new home was located. Behind him, Maria was still as chatty as ever, but at this point, Mandy paid no mind to her. The only thought on his mind was Hamza. He wondered how he'd cope. Would he be able to survive without the privileged lifestyle he had been used to? Would he be able to lay low, or would he get tired of the condescending treatment he'd get from people and reveal who he really was someday? "God forbid!" he murmured.

He cringed at the thought of his little brother opening up to the wrong people, people who would betray him and divulge information to their uncle.

At that moment, Mandy regretted his action at the refugee center. He shouldn't have flipped out the way he did. He should have been more courteous. He should have asked that woman to please tell him which city she was taking Hamza to. He should have asked for the phone number of the new foster parents. He should have appealed to her emotions instead of letting his frustrations get the better of him. He needed to have better control over his emotions. He wished he could go back and fix things, but since that was impossible, what Mandy needed now was a computer with an Internet connection. He needed to send Hamza an email, hoping that he, too, would get access to a computer very soon and reply to his message so they could find a way to reunite.

After climbing the seemingly endless stairs to the fifth floor, they walked down a long, airless hallway, which led to an old wooden door with hastily applied brown oil paint shimmering against the bright white light on the ceiling. Mandy could swear that they had painted the door because of him, and he wondered what other stress they might have gone through just to impress him and why they had thought it necessary to do any of it. After all, he felt like he was the one who needed to put up an impressive performance so they wouldn't have any reason to send him away.

Andrew fiddled with the keys for a while before the door gave way and they walked into a nearly dark apartment. Andrew reached for the light switch on the wall. He pressed it up and down a few times, but the light refused to come on.

"Seems the light has some issues," Maria chirped.

"I'll get an electrician to fix it," Andrew promised and asked Mandy to follow him as he dragged his luggage into one of the rooms.

"This is your room, Mandy," he said and dropped the backpack on a small reading table beside the door. He opened the drawer by the table and brought out a small flashlight. "You can freshen up, rest a while, and come out for dinner later. Okay? The light will come on soon."

"Okay." Mandy nodded, and Andrew left the room.

Mandy kicked his shoes off, lay on the bed, shut his eyes, and yawned. He was so hungry and tired. He could hear Andrew and Maria arguing about the light bills. He couldn't hear them clearly, but he could hear them enough to know that Andrew hadn't been able to pay the light bill earlier because he hadn't gotten some money he was expecting. Their faint voices filtered into Mandy's ears for a while before he drifted off to sleep, a much-needed rest that was cut short when the bright light from the halogen bulb on the ceiling came on.

Mandy sat and started checking out the room. He took in everything—from the fading cream color on the walls to the tiny mattress wrapped with a neatly ironed sky-blue sheet decorated with pictures of Harry Potter with a flying broom stuck between his legs and one hand stretched out holding a magic wand. The room lacked space. It was as if the walls were uncomfortable being that close to each other. Mandy walked to the only window and opened it to let in some air to quell the stuffiness hanging in the room.

"Do you like your new room?" Maria's voice rang out as she opened the door and barged in.

"Yeah, I do," Mandy lied.

He wished he could tell her that he didn't like being snuck up on and that the least they could do to help him get used to living in a room smaller than his bathroom in Sikasso was to give him a little space to collect his thoughts, a little space to squeeze himself between the sheets and cry until his eyes became bloodshot and his voice became too frayed to say a word. But Maria was not one to read body language. She came and stood by him at the window and looked outside at the children playing basketball on a small court down the street.

"The view is magnificent, don't you think?"

"Indeed it is," Mandy said between clenched teeth.

"Alright, come out for dinner later. I'm making fried rice and chicken." She patted him on the shoulder and walked out of the room.

At the dinner table, Mandy could not help but wonder if he shouldn't just cut to the chase and tell them that

Africa wasn't the cave they thought it was. They set a spoon beside the fork and knife near his plate of fried rice. Maria, Andrew, and their twelve-year-old daughter, Alice, kept staring at Musa as he picked up the fork and knife.

"I'll show you how to use those," Maria said, moving her seat back and trying to stand up.

"Don't worry, I got it," Mandy said and began to eat.

They kept looking at him silently as they ate. Mandy knew they were waiting for him to make one gaffe that would prove whatever things they thought they knew about Africa.

When he retired to his room that night, Mandy's heart was heavy. There were so many things he wanted to say, so many tears he wanted to let out, but no one he could talk to. Although Maria had asked him a thousand times already to talk to her about anything, he knew he couldn't open up to her or anyone in the house. He did like her, though he wished she would talk less and listen a little more. Still, to be safe and start a new life in America, it was best for him to keep calm, accept his fate, and be Mandy Patrick.

He picked up a pen on the table and began to write on a notepad.

From the bed to the floor, from the skies to the murky waters,

Life takes us through turns we can't predict.

One day you're a prince, with servants throwing petals at your feet,

But the sun falls and rises; and you find yourself scrambling through the woods,

Looking for an unfortunate grasshopper, to snap its head off and feed your churning stomach.

One day a whole city bows at the mention of your name, but you snap out of the daydream your life has been, and you can't even say your name anymore.

When the journey gets rough and a thousand enemies are lurking behind you, all you need to do is survive.

Breath is the essence of life, and a wise man would choose it above any other.

Even if it means throwing your name away, just breathe, for that's the one sane thing to do.

Breathe, just breathe! And the only way to breathe right now is to embrace this life with hands open wide.

And say, "Dear Musa, it was nice being you; now let's say hello to Mandy Patrick."

Chapter Seventeen

"Musa! Musa!" Musa heard Hamza cry out. Musa searched everywhere, trying to figure out where the sound was coming from. He was standing at the edge of a river, and there was no one in sight apart from a lone fisherman paddling his canoe in the middle of the river. The shouting continued. Hamza's voice rang out so loud that it echoed into the waters.

"Hamza, where are you? Hamza!" Musa yelled back.

He turned around and listened carefully. It seemed like the sound was coming from an abandoned building by the riverbank. The old house was surrounded by a makeshift fence built with rusty-brown zinc roofing sheets. Musa ran to the fence and pressed his ear against the roofing sheets.

"Musa, help me! Help me!" Hamza's voice cried again. This time faintly, as if he had no more energy left in him.

"Hamza, I am coming," Musa screamed.

He started to run around the fence, looking for an entrance until he saw a small door. He threw his weight against the door, forced it open, and ran inside. As soon as Musa's feet touched the ground inside the compound, he felt a heavy force pulling at his legs, making it impossible for him to move. The ground underneath him was muddy, and as he struggled to pull his legs out and jump to the dry land a few inches in front of him, he felt himself sinking further.

"Musa, he's going to kill me. He's going to kill me."

The agony in Hamza's voice broke Musa's heart into a thousand pieces. He pulled his leg harder, but he was stuck and sinking so deep that the mud was already up to his knee. As Musa continued trying to pull himself out of the thick sinking mud, he looked around and saw a plank dug into the ground in front of him. He reached out and held on to the plank. He shook the plank a little to see if it would break, but it was strongly rooted. He tightened his grip on the plank and forced his right leg out of the mud and onto dry land. Then he pulled the other leg out and ran to the entrance of the building, lumps of mud dropping from his stained trousers.

Musa forced the door open and stormed into the dark room, which had no light source apart from the door through which he had entered. The floor of the room was stained with grease and oil. Empty containers of engine lubricants, rusty metal rings, and old car wheels were scattered all around the room, and the choking smell of a burning car engine hung in the air. Musa grabbed a metal pipe he could use as a weapon.

"Hamza, are you there? Hamza!" He walked inside slowly, eyes darting to the left and right, legs quivering in fear and heart pounding loudly in his chest.

"Hamza? Hamza!"

No sound came forth.

Suddenly, the door snapped shut, and pitch darkness covered the room.

"No! No! No!" Musa screamed and ran toward the door. Suddenly, a heavy plank landed on his back. He screamed out. The plank hit him again, and he fell on the ground. Then he heard the sound of a switch, and a bright light came on.

He saw the face of his attacker. It was his uncle, Abdulsalaam Mahmoud. He dropped the plank on the ground and laughed out loud.

"Look who we have here," Abdulsalaam jeered, smiling wickedly and rubbing his palms in glee.

"Uncle Abdul, why? Why are you doing this? What have we ever done to make you hate us so much? What do you want from us?" Musa cried.

"To send you where you belong. Where you should have been a very long time ago." Abdulsalaam pulled a dagger from his belt and walked closer to Musa, who was lying on the ground, pleading for his life.

"Uncle, please. Please don't do it," Musa pleaded.

Abdulsalaam's ears were deaf to the boy's pleas. With his hand tightly gripped around the hilt of the dagger, he raised the weapon to thrust into Musa's chest. Musa screamed.

Mandy snapped his eyes open. He was shivering and sweating, and tears poured from his eyes. The door flew open and Maria ran in. She sat on the bed and held his hand.

"Calm down, Mandy. Calm down. It was just a dream," she said. Then Andrew walked in and leaned against the doorframe, watching as his wife wiped the sweat off Mandy's forehead.

"He had a nightmare again," she said, looking at Andrew. Andrew shook his head in pity. Mandy had been having nightmares every night since he got there.

* * *

Unlike Maria, Andrew didn't say much. Instead of speaking, he preferred to watch intensely, shake his head when he disapproved of something, or give a weak smile when something caught his fancy. Mandy had never heard him laugh loudly. Sometimes Mandy felt that Andrew also needed space from Maria but couldn't ask for it. He had this feeling especially during the times when Andrew would be sitting on the couch watching a TV show and Maria would come and lie next to him with her head on his lap and her legs on the armrest. She would giggle and laugh at every scene and conversation, and her eyes would expectantly flicker toward Andrew, seemingly hoping that he too would catch the joke and laugh with her. He would just manage to scoff or grin or put on what Mandy called a "solidarity smile"—smiling out of courtesy, not because he had a genuine reason to smile.

There was one other thing that fueled Mandy's suspicion that Andrew was a ticking time bomb. It was the fact that Maria was easily the man of the house. Mandy was not naive to the fact that women in the Western world were nothing like the ones in Africa, who worshipped their husbands and extolled the sand upon which they left their footprints. Although he hadn't lived with or had the chance to observe any Western family before now, he had watched enough movies and read enough books to know that equality was the trademark of their union. In Maria and Andrew's case, however, it was totally different. Andrew sat on the fence in so many conversations and nodded anytime Maria made a decision.

Andrew was a retired military man. Mandy's eyes had gone wide in surprise when he heard this. Andrew looked no more than forty-five years old. Alice, the couple's daughter, told him this.

Mandy was looking at the pictures on the wall in the living room. Beside a picture of the couple smiling happily with little Alice stuck in between them was a picture of Andrew wearing a military uniform.

"Daddy looked good in his uniform, right?" Alice's voice asked from behind him.

He turned around and saw her looking at him with proud eyes.

"Yeah? Yeah," Mandy stammered. "I didn't know he is a soldier."

"He was. He's now a veteran. He is retired," Alice retorted. She opened a small drawer on a table by the wall and brought out their family photo album. They sat on the couch, and she began to show him more pictures. There were many more pictures of Andrew wearing military uniforms.

"But why did he retire? He still looks so young," Mandy asked.

Alice laughed hysterically, like someone who just remembered something very funny. "I bet you don't want to know," she said.

"Of course, I do," Mandy said.

"Daddy shot himself in the leg just to retire," the little girl said and burst into laughter again.

Now Mandy was lost. It didn't make any sense to him, and he wondered if Alice was just being like her mother, laughing at almost everything.

When she caught her breath and stopped laughing, Alice narrated the story to him.

Andrew worked with the military for many years, and his team recorded many successful operations. In all of his years in the military, Andrew always found a way to hide in the background on the battlefield. He would hide at the safest points he could and shoot mainly to defend himself from the enemy, not to launch an assault. They had the most tactical shooters on their team, so it was easy for him to hide his cowardice in the shadow of their bravery.

One day, a letter arrived from the Pentagon. His team had been reshuffled into different teams; some of them had been promoted, and they were given new assignments. Andrew was assigned to lead his new team on a peacekeeping mission in the war-torn Democratic Republic of Congo. Andrew was scared to the bone. He came back home that night looking depressed. He would neither touch his food nor come to the living room to be with his wife and daughter. He just took his shower and lay in bed, tossing about restlessly. Maria probed him all night before he dropped the bombshell.

"Oh my God! What are you going to do now?" Maria had asked.

"I can't go. I can't waste my life fighting a fight that is not even mine," he said. "I can't leave you both here and put my life on the forefront of that battle."

According to the little girl, Maria knew that Andrew spoke more out of cowardice than he did for the love of his family, but she encouraged him, telling him she believed in him and knew he would come back alive. But that wasn't what he wanted to hear. He wanted her to cry and to beg him not to go, but it seemed like she didn't care what happened to him. Andrew ignored her and perfected his plans. The next day the family received a call from the training facility that there had been an accident. They said Andrew's gun had gone off mistakenly and shot him in the leg.

Andrew was in the hospital while his squad left for the peacekeeping mission, and on that hospital bed, he thought deeply about his career. He couldn't continue living this fake life. He applied for retirement, and after he recovered, he began driving a delivery truck. Alice said she and Maria still made fun of him from time to time whenever they remembered the story.

As Mandy and Alice looked through the photo album, the excited girl had something to say about every picture. Although Mandy smiled and tried to pay attention to the girl, he had just one question on his mind.

"Alice, is that computer functional?" he asked.

"Yes," she said. "Do you want to see my scores on Sudoku?" She jumped up from the couch and went to turn on the computer. As the computer came on, the girl opened her Sudoku game and started showing off her numbers.

"Wow, that's impressive. Do you mind if I check something really quickly?" Mandy grabbed the mouse and pulled up the Internet settings. "Alice, there's no Internet connection?"

"No, I don't think so. I heard Mom and Dad talking about it yesterday. Mom says it's Dad's turn to pay the Internet bills. Dad said he doesn't have the money yet."

Mandy shook his head. He wondered why this couple had graciously volunteered to take him in when they could barely pay their own bills. He felt sad that he couldn't help them pay some bills. If they could be this benevolent when they didn't even have enough money to live a comfortable life, how much more could they be when their finances improved? At that very moment, Mandy made up his mind that if he ever got back what he had lost, he would make sure this family never lacked for anything.

* * *

Saturdays were for cleaning in Mandy's new family. Andrew was to vacuum the living room, and Alice and Mandy were to clean their rooms, while Maria scrubbed the kitchen.

Mandy picked up a broom and went into the bedroom. He closed the door behind him and looked at the rumpled bed sheets and the floor littered with papers, cookie wrappers, and various dust and debris. He held the stalk of the broom and tried to recall whether he had consciously watched any of the servants at home using it before. He thought so hard, but he couldn't remember having ever watched them. He had always seen them walking around the palace with brooms and other such things in the morning, but he never once wondered what they were doing with them.

"Alice, Mandy, hurry up, guys. I need some help down here," Maria called from the kitchen.

Mandy pressed the bristles firmly against the floor and tried to push the dirt with it. He heard Alice's voice say that she was almost done. He continued pressing the bristles against the floor and brushing it against the carpet until he felt the broom crack. He pressed harder, and the handle broke.

"Oh my God, what have I done?" he cried. Just then, the door opened and Maria entered.

"Are you still cleaning this room, Mandy?" she asked. She looked around the dirty room; the small wardrobe was open, and clothes were scattered all around. "What have you been doing?"

Mandy cast his face to the ground. He suddenly couldn't look her in the eyes. "I was trying to use the broom, but it broke."

"Oh, I hope it didn't injure you," Maria said. She took the broom from him. "You don't know how to use a broom?"

Mandy shook his head.

"Oh dear. I'm sorry. I should have shown you. This isn't the type you use in Africa?" she asked.

She bent down to sweep with the half of the broom fixed to the bristles. Mandy watched as she swept half of the room, and then she gave him back the broom and watched as he completed the task.

Apart from her constant condescending remarks about Africa, Maria was a kind woman. Initially, Mandy didn't like her because she was so talkative, but the way she took care of him during his nightmares had made his resentment towards her fade away. There were nights when he would jerk up from a bad dream, and before he opened his eyes, he would see Maria holding his hand and telling him everything would be alright. Later in the day, she would ask him to tell her about the nightmares, but Mandy would not tell her that it was the image of his uncle firing bullets into his father's chest that haunted him. He would not tell her that he always saw his uncle chasing and trying to kill him and his brother. He would claim that it was about the trauma he felt when he almost died in the Mediterranean.

Some days after his first nightmare, Maria came home from work with a plastic bag filled with novels. She said she had driven past a yard sale on her way, so she decided to buy some books for Mandy. She said that reading the novels would help create new images in his mind, which would drown out the tragic events haunting him. She said she knew he needed therapy, but they couldn't afford it at the moment, but as soon as school started and he made new friends, he would get over the trauma.

Maria watched him sweep for a while. Then she shook her head and started teaching him again. She taught him how to hold the edge of the broom and swipe the bristles gently yet firmly against the floor, sweeping the dirt along. When they were done cleaning up the room, they went to the kitchen.

"Mommy, Mandy can't wash dishes," Alice said, laughing.

Shadows of Exile

"Wow, Mandy, really?" She was dumbfounded.

Mandy felt uneasy. How could he explain to these people that this was his first time doing any chores? He wondered if this was the right time for him to open up to them. Would they believe his story? If they did, what kind of help could they offer him apart from empathy? He hated pity, and he feared that Maria would share the story with her colleagues, and maybe somehow, just somehow, the news would get into the wrong ears. Worse still, what if he told them his story and they didn't believe him? What if they told him his story was stale, just like the Spaniards did?

"Mandy, you also don't wash dishes in Africa?" Maria asked.

"My sisters did the dishes and other housework. I only helped my father on the farm and in his stall," Mandy blurted. He hoped that claiming to be good at farming would make them realize he wasn't entirely useless.

"Oh, you can farm? That's so cute. Maybe someday when I have enough space to have a garden, you'd help me out there."

"Sure," Mandy chirped, watching with rapt attention as Alice did the dishes.

As the weeks passed, Mandy became more acquainted with his new family. He had waited patiently all the while, hoping Maria and Andrew would pay their Internet bills so he could use the computer to send Hamza an email, but the couple seemed to have other things to do with their money. From his room, which was just across from theirs, he heard them having heated conversations that always revolved around money.

"I am very sure of these numbers. The guy who gave them to my friend has won over a million dollars," Mandy overheard Andrew saying one rainy night.

"You say this all the time." Maria's voice was a little louder. "Every other week you claim to get numbers from this angel or the other angel, yet you never win a single cent! Now how are we going to pay all of these bills if you keep throwing money around like this?"

Lying in his bed, looking at the water splashing against the window, Mandy shook his head. He felt bad to be an extra burden on the shoulders of this poor couple.

Since he couldn't get access to the Internet yet, Mandy often stayed glued to the TV whenever the couple wasn't at home. He would scroll from one news channel to the other, hoping to stumble on any news concerning the situation in Mali, but there was nothing. It seemed like they were either deliberately quiet about the murder of his father or he just hadn't tuned in on time.

One day, Alice sat on the carpet in the center of the living room doing her schoolwork. Mandy came into the living room and squatted beside her.

"What are you writing?" he asked.

"It's my vacation project. They asked us to write five essays on these topics." She passed him a paper that listed the topics.

"Oh wow, that's quite a lot. So how many have you written?"

"This is the second one. It's difficult," she whined.

"Can I help you?"

Alice was excited. "Yeah!" She paused for a moment. "But do you know how to write an essay?"

"Well, let's find out."

Mandy and the girl sat at the dining table and started working. Mandy came up with the ideas and taught Alice how to write proper essays that would surprise her teacher.

Maria was impressed when she walked in and saw them. She read one of the essays and then turned to Mandy with her mouth wide open. "Mandy! How is it that you write this good?"

"But I didn't write that; Alice did."

"Oh, please, spare me the modesty." Maria waved his denial away. "This is really impressive. What class were you in before you left home?"

Mandy thought for a while. Was this the right time to tell her the truth? Would she believe him if he told her his real academic status? It seemed unlikely, so he shrugged. "I was just about to start college."

"Wow! So why didn't you just stay back? You're clearly a bright student! Who knows, maybe you would have gotten a scholarship."

Mandy told her that Africa wasn't like America where bright students were appreciated so much. He once again told her the story of how his parents were too poor to care for him and his eleven siblings, so he had to join some other young people to get on a boat going to Europe.

Chapter Eighteen

Mandy hurried down the tiled hallway and took a left into the school computer lab. He didn't say a word to any of the students hanging around exchanging pleasantries and catching up with each other after the long summer holiday. He saw a few eyes staring at him as he walked toward the lab, but he had no time to return their glances or try to make friends. He had only one thing on his mind.

"Good morning, ma'am." He smiled at the attendant as soon as he entered the computer lab.

"Good morning. How may I help you?"

"I'd like to use the computers, please."

"Are you new here?" The woman gave him a strange look.

"Yeah, it's my first day here."

"Oh, I see. Feel free to use any of the computers over there." She pointed at the left side of the room. There were over a hundred computers in the room, and he could see students using some of them.

The woman pointed to the right side. "This other side is for staff only. Your student password won't work on there."

Mandy thanked the woman and headed to the last computer at the end of the room, just beside the wall. He logged into his email and scrolled down, hoping to see a message from Hamza. He had seventy-three unread messages, but none of them was from his brother.

"Oh God, I hope Hamza is fine. God, please," he murmured, and wiped at the tears that had already formed. He clicked on the new mail icon and started typing.

Hello Hamza,

I hope this finds you well. First of all, I am sorry for not being there with you. I am sorry for the way I reacted when the Spanish authorities came to pick you up. I should have been calmer and asked them to at least give me the address of the place they were taking you.

How have you been? I hope your foster family is nice and you're coping quite well. I am in New York, and it has been so difficult trying to adjust to this new life.

Hamza, please be careful out there. Always remember that being on Father's throne has made Uncle Abdul so powerful that he could still have eyes and ears out there trying to seek us out. Please do your best to stay low-key for now. However, please reach out to me. Send me your address or a phone number I can call to reach you.

Shadows of Exile

I have been thinking, and I have come up with some ideas of things we can do to get back some of the things we lost. However, I need to see you first before I make any moves. I need to be sure you are fine and secure before I do anything.

Please reach out to me as soon as possible.

I love you always,

Musa

After sending the email, Mandy started reading through his log of unread messages. They were messages from his friends, who were in shock over the news they heard. Some of them texted to confirm that what they heard wasn't true; others wanted to know if he survived the attack. A few sent "Rest in Peace" and some other condolence messages that made him wonder if they expected him to read their messages somehow from the land of the dead. Mandy then went on Google and typed in "king of Mali killed" and found lots of news websites had carried the news, describing it as a bloody coup. One of the headlines caught his attention. It read, "New Malian King Swears to Avenge His Brother's Death." Mandy quickly clicked on the article.

The new Malian king, Mansa Abdulsalaam Mahmoud, has sworn to avenge the death of his brother. The monarch made this declaration last week during a chat with newsmen during an inspection tour of the country's new gold refinery, Mansa Pure Stones. The monarch announced that he has received a briefing from the detectives and a panel of inquiry he set up to investigate the murder.

"What nonsense!" Mandy blurted, and slammed his fist against the table.

"Hey, man, are you okay?" a voice asked, and he looked up from the computer to see several eyes looking in his direction.

He mumbled an apology and quickly logged out of the computer.

Mandy couldn't pay attention in class. He spent the whole time wondering how his uncle could be so deceptive. How could he set up a panel of inquiry into a crime he had committed? The words "panel of inquiry" kept ringing in his head. He feared that the panel had a hidden agenda, that maybe the panel was actually set up to find him and Hamza. He remembered that it was customary for the kings of Sikasso to have spies and messengers lurking around their children abroad, and he wondered if maybe the panel of inquiry were in fact spies that had been scattered around the world to hunt them down.

Suddenly, Mandy became self-conscious. He looked at the students around him, from the blonde girl at the desk next to his, making notes on her book as the teacher taught, to the round red-haired boy behind him. "What if one of these kids is a spy?" he wondered. His eyes darted from one face to the other. He could feel his heart pounding in his chest and goose bumps popping up all over his body. He stood up and grabbed his backpack.

"Hey, where are you going?" the teacher asked. The whole class turned around to look at Mandy.

"Umm...the bathroom?"

The teacher looked at Mandy keenly for a while, as if he were trying to reconcile the face with an image in his mind. "I can't recall seeing you before. Are you new here?"

"Yes, sir. It's my first day," Mandy said.

"Oh, I see." The teacher walked toward Mandy. The man was tall; he had well-chiseled cheekbones and broad shoulders, which gave him an intimidating aura. Mandy's heart pounded faster as the man got closer. Could this be it? Could this man be one of the men looking for him?

"What's your name?" the man asked.

"Musa!" he blurted. "Sorry. It's Mandy. Mandy Patrick"

"Are you trying to guess your name?" the teacher asked. The class giggled.

"No, sir. My name is Mandy Patrick. The other name is just a nickname."

"Oh, a nickname. Do you want to tell us your nickname?"

Mandy shook his head.

"Where are you from?"

"Ivory Coast," Mandy said. His eyes were fixed on the teacher, hoping they wouldn't ask more questions.

The teacher walked back toward the front of the class. "Can anyone point at Ivory Coast on the map?" he asked, pointing at the large world map on the wall.

One of the students raised her hand. The teacher asked her to speak. "It's somewhere in Africa," she said.

"Yeah." The teacher nodded. "But can you locate it on the map?"

As the girl tried to figure it out, another student blurted from somewhere behind Mandy, "I thought Africa was a country."

"No, it's a continent," the teacher retorted. "So, what else do you know about it?" The teacher focused back at the girl.

"Well, not much. I see it on National Geographic."

"So, do you all run around naked and have lions and tigers as pets?" another boy asked, looking at Mandy. The whole class laughed.

Embarrassed, Mandy walked out of the class. He rushed into the bathroom and splashed some water on his face. He looked in the mirror, took several deep breaths, and tried to calm his frayed nerves.

* * *

Mandy's first two weeks in school were tough. He was constantly afraid someone was watching him. His fears and insecurity caused him to isolate himself from the other students. He would rather stay in the computer lab reading every news article he could find about his home country and sending email after email to Hamza than hang out with the other boys at the basketball court.

He sent over one hundred emails to Hamza but didn't get a single email in response. He feared that the worst could have happened to his brother. Every morning and night he prayed for God to protect his little brother, and he comforted himself with the knowledge that the spirits of their late parents were on guard over them.

Chapter Nineteen

Mandy sat at a table in the school cafeteria talking with Brian, Debbie, and Carlos about their group's history project. Debbie had looked so excited the day the teacher called out the groups. As soon as Professor Benard's class was over and the students started leaving the class, Debbie rushed over to Mandy's seat. She had tried being friends with Mandy for some time, but Mandy hadn't met her overtures with enthusiasm. Something about her didn't sit right with him. She was fair-skinned, slim, and beautiful, with upper and lower gaps in her teeth, which were noticeable each time she smiled, but her beauty didn't appeal to Mandy. Mandy had seen how friendly she was with other students, but he still felt uncomfortable around her and always replied to her attempts to talk to him in forced monosyllables. He had tried to figure out what exactly he didn't like about her, but it was hard for him to decide if it was because she was dating Bobby, one of the most notorious bullies in the school, or because she was nosy. Unlike the other students, who cautiously said hi and went back to their seats, on Mandy's first day of school, Debbie had so many questions about Africa; questions

Mandy carefully ignored. He wanted to keep a low profile and to keep his interactions with other students to a minimum to avoid drawing attention to himself. If anyone was going to put two and two together, though, it was Debbie.

Debbie saw the perfect opportunity she had been looking for. She walked up to Mandy, pulled a seat close to him, and settled into it.

"Look, I know you're not always comfortable around me," she started, "so before the other group members come over, I'd like us to be clear on something. Do you think we can work together on this project as friends, or should I just ask Professor Benard to assign me to another group? I promise I won't tell him my reasons."

Mandy saw the sincerity in her eyes. Now that he looked at her closely, she seemed harmless.

"No, Debbie, I don't have a problem with you," Mandy said. "I just—"

"You just don't like that I ask so many questions, right? I understand. I was just curious to know a little bit more about Africa. I've read a bunch of African literature, and I was excited to maybe get a chance to become friends with someone from Africa, who'd tell me about their culture. I didn't really mean to bother you."

"Oh, I see. Well, there is a lot more to Africa than what you see on National Geographic. It's not just huts and safaris. There are beautiful modern cities just like here. Bobby is wrong about Africa, and he thinks there is something going on between us."

As the team went through the books where they had made notes from their individual research, Bobby and his friend Dejuan popped into the cafeteria. Mandy watched as the boys looked around like they were searching for someone.

"Debbie, I think he's looking for you," Mandy said and gestured toward Bobby.

Debbie waved at Bobby. He and his friend started toward them. As soon as Bobby saw Mandy, the smile on his face wrinkled into a frown.

"Yo! Whatcha doing with this guy all the time?" he snapped at Debbie.

"Hey, chill out. I told you we're working on a project."

"What lousy project? And why does it have to be with village boy?" He pointed at Mandy.

Debbie stood up angrily. "Stop it, Bobby! What the hell is wrong with you?"

Everyone in the cafeteria had turned to look at them. Mandy held Debbie's hand. "Come on, Debbie, it's okay. Don't create a scene."

"Get your filthy hands off my girl!" Bobby barked and quickly slapped Mandy's hand away from Debbie's.

The slap stung. Mandy was enraged. He stood up and pointed at Bobby's face. "Don't ever touch me again, Bobby."

"Or what?" Bobby challenged him. "Or what?" Bobby shoved him.

"Bobby!" Debbie called.

"I'm warning you for the last time, Bobby. Don't touch me."

"Or you'll do what?" Bobby shoved Mandy again.

Mandy staggered back. He clenched his right fist and furiously punched Bobby on the jaw. Bobby reeled back, and before he could regain his balance, Mandy grabbed him by both shoulders and pushed him so hard that he crashed against one of the tables.

Everyone in the cafeteria cheered. Dejuan ran to Bobby's aid and pulled him up, and they quickly ran out of the cafeteria in shame. The students started clapping for him, while Mandy looked around surprised at himself. It was the first time anyone had ever challenged Bobby. As Mandy basked in the euphoria of the moment, he saw two students, a boy and a girl, recording the scene with their mobile phones.

"Hey, come here. May I see that?" He beckoned at both students.

The students excitedly brought him their phones, and Mandy immediately deleted the videos.

"Thank you very much. But I don't want anyone seeing that on the internet."

He gave them their phones back. Although he felt like a local hero, the euphoria of the moment wouldn't make him forget that he needed to keep a low profile and that having a video of him out on the internet might put him in trouble.

* * *

School ended for the semester, and Mandy was back to staying at home. One evening, as Mandy lay in bed reading a novel, Maria called him to join them in the living room. The couple looked so excited. They announced that the school had just sent them an email with Mandy's grades. He had "A"s in all his courses.

"We are so proud of you, Mandy," Maria chirped.

"Thank you." Mandy was humbled, but he wasn't as excited as the couple. If only they knew that everything they taught in that school was stuff he already knew.

Maria went on to tell him that the school had also said in the email that he had been chosen to compete in the National High School Quiz Competition. They told him that the top three contestants from last year won college scholarships.

"Wow. That's so cool!" Mandy said. This was his opportunity to finally get ahead and maybe get a better life. At least he would get some financial support so that he could stop being a burden to his foster parents. As Mandy reveled in the daydream of a better life, something hit him. How did Maria and Andrew know what the kids from last year's competition win?

"Do they show the competition on TV?" he asked.

"Yes, boy. On almost every TV station," Andrew replied. There was an obvious pride in Andrew's voice.

Mandy knew that they expected that he would be excited to appear on TV, but he shook his head. "I am sorry. I can't go."

"What?" Maria could not believe her ears. "Come on; you can do this. Don't be scared. Just take a look at your excellent results. You have what it takes."

"I know. But I just can't go. If it's going to be shown on TV, then I won't be able to go."

"But why? What's wrong with being on TV?" Maria's voice was growing loud.

"Nothing. I just can't be on TV. Let's just say that I am camera shy."

"You don't have to be!" Maria insisted. She urged him to forget about the cameras and focus on the prize, that this was his chance, but Mandy remained adamant. Maria flipped. "You have to do it! You have to go do this competition. Did you risk your life on the sea only to get to America and throw away opportunities? Well, I won't let you!" she snapped.

"You won't understand." Mandy was lost for words. "I just can't be out there on TV. I just can't be."

Mandy was at a crossroads. He figured that maybe this was the right time for him to tell them the truth. Before he could begin, however, Maria exploded.

"I am not going to let you have this opportunity pass us by! You think if we knew they were going to pay us peanuts for your upkeep, that we would have taken you in?"

"Maria!" Andrew called. "It's okay!"

But Maria wouldn't stop. "You think it's easy for us around here? You see food to eat every day without paying any bills, and now you get the opportunity to do something that would maybe bring us some more money, and you want to screw it up? I won't let you do that. So you better go to your room, think about this, and make up your mind to be in that competition."

Mandy was dumbfounded. He couldn't believe that Maria would speak to him that way. He couldn't believe that all these months it had been all about the money. He realized how wrong he had been to think that she genuinely cared about him. As he walked back into his room, the tears flowed. It was going to be a long night of thinking of what to do next. The competition was to happen in one month. He prayed that that would be enough time to find a way to make them change their minds.

Shadows of Exile

Chapter Twenty

The few positive feelings Mandy had started to have toward his new home quickly evaporated. After their altercation, Maria became very hostile to Mandy, saying only the bare minimum to him. At the slightest provocation, she would flip out. Alice had traveled to visit her grandmother for the two-week break, so Mandy had no one to talk to. He had read all the novels he had, so he turned back to his first love—writing.

Most days, the only bit of happiness he had was when Maria and Andrew were at work. He would stay home alone, doing the load of chores Maria would command him to do, after which he would watch TV and secretly use the computer to read Malian news and send more emails to Hamza. Once it was time for Maria to come home from work, he would delete his browsing history and return to his room. He would then walk on tenterhooks until they left for work the next day.

One Saturday night, Andrew and Maria were both in the living room when Mandy went from his room to the kitchen to get a drink of water. Maria was at the computer desk, completing some proposals she needed to present to her boss on Monday, while Andrew was on the sofa, his eyes glued to the TV. From the kitchen Mandy could hear the newscaster announce their next headline: "Brutal Dictatorship Escalates in Mali as New King Orders Execution of Three Councilmen." Mandy quickly walked to the kitchen doorway from where he could see the TV clearly.

> *Political tension thickens in the West African country of Mali as the new monarch, Mansa Abdul Salaam II, has ordered the immediate execution of three councilmen, who were accused of treachery and other undisclosed treasonable felonies. Since the pronouncement on Tuesday, there have been widespread protests in the royal city of Sikasso, many of which were disrupted by military personnel who shot tear gas to disperse the protesting civilians.*

At this point, Maria looked up from her computer to the TV screen, where footage of people carrying picket signs, and clashes with police forces were being shown.

> *This comes as a surprise to most observers, as the condemned councilmen are members of the new council set up by the king after he came to power a few months ago following the brutal murder of his brother and late monarch, Mansa Idris. Malian citizens have cried out to the United Nations and other relevant foreign*

bodies to intervene, to stop the wanton killing perpetrated by the monarch, who is suspected to have sponsored the bloody massacre of his brother, King Idris, and hundreds of royal guards and servants. The fate of the queen and the two heirs, Prince Musa and Prince Hamza, remains unknown. They are presumed dead, although their bodies have not been found.

As the anchorman read the concluding parts, they flashed pictures of King Idris, the queen, Musa, and Hamza on the screen.

Mandy's heart skipped a beat.

"Oh my God! Oh my God!" Maria shouted. "Andrew, that's Mandy."

Andrew looked at her like she was crazy. "What are you talking about?"

"I said, 'That's Mandy.' The older kid in that family picture they just showed."

"Which Mandy are you talking about?"

"Mandy. Our Mandy!" she said in a hushed tone and pointed toward Mandy's room.

It still didn't make sense to Andrew. The idea seemed ridiculous.

"Mandy is Musa. The son of the king they just talked about. That's him," Maria insisted.

"Why would you think something so ridiculous? Your foster kid is an African prince? That's hilarious." Andrew laughed and turned back to the TV.

Maria moved next to Andrew and explained that she had suspected Mandy was hiding something. She asked Andrew whether he hadn't found it surprising that they had to teach Mandy everything about chores like he was a kid.

"Yeah, I was surprised, but I thought maybe we picked a lazy African child. Besides, he said he farms. But then again, it didn't make sense," Andrew concurred.

"Yes!" She seemed happy that he was beginning to reason the way she wanted him to. "But I don't think that was the case," Maria continued. "I think he couldn't do those things because he had people doing them for him!"

Andrew seemed lost.

"You see," Maria said, "one day, I found a note in his closet. Let me get it."

Mandy hid behind the kitchen door. Maria ran into their bedroom and came out with a piece of paper. Mandy recognized the paper. It was from the notepad he'd used when he wrote his first poem the day he came to live with them.

Andrew read through the contents of the paper, but he still wasn't convinced. "What if this is just a coincidence? You know this kid is good with his pen. What if he was just being creative?"

"Andrew, look beyond that and see the obvious. First, he was a totally spoiled brat who couldn't even sweep his room or wash the dishes, but he can do every cool thing kids do. That alone points to the fact that he had people doing everything for him. Remember he always changes the topic whenever we talk about him reaching out to his family? And now one missing prince happens to share the name he used to have according to this piece he wrote."

She gave Andrew the kind of look you'd give a dunce when they give you reasons to wonder if they really do have a brain in their skull.

"Let's check the internet and look at that picture again," Andrew said.

They got on the computer and typed in the website of the television station and scrolled down to the news. "Oh my God! This is unbelievable," Andrew said.

"What do we do now?" Maria asked.

"I don't know," he said, tapping his fingers on the table and pacing around the room.

"But we have to do something," Maria said. "He needs to tell us the truth about who he really is."

"Yeah," Andrew concurred, "and he should also tell us what he really has. I mean, even if he did escape the palace during the coup, he wouldn't be totally penniless. This kid may be hiding a gold mine under all that poor-boy bullshit he's fronting."

Maria paused for a moment.

"Wow! Now everything makes sense. Remember the way he reacted when we told him about the quiz competition?"

"Yes, yes!"

"He did that because he's scared of being seen on TV. Maybe his uncle thinks he's dead, and he wants it to remain that way until he's ready to go back."

"Hmm, now I see. Smart kid!" Andrew nodded. "If he's scared to go on TV, he is scared that his uncle might see him. He still feels threatened. That's why he wants to lay low."

"Exactly! So, what do we do now?"

"We have to draw him closer. Think about this. This kid must have a lot of money in his name. Maybe he's just waiting for the right time to make use of it, or maybe he's waiting to get to a certain age. We have to embrace him now, make him realize that we know his story, promise to protect him, and then, boom, he lets his guard down and we get access to some of that money."

"And what if he doesn't agree? What if he doesn't trust us enough to take the bait?"

"We threaten him!"

Mandy's heart skipped a beat again. His legs and body were quivering with fear. He was scared that once again he had landed in an enemy zone. When the couple returned to the sofa to work out their scheme, he tiptoed back to his room.

Holding the doorknob behind him, Mandy felt his heart sinking deep. This was the end of the road for him. He sat on the bed and thought for a while. It was dangerous to remain in this house. Andrew and Maria had revealed their true selves. How would he tell them that he couldn't access any of his family's fortunes? How could he even trust that they would believe that he came out empty-handed? He thought of trying to explain to them everything that happened that night, but when he remembered the excitement on their faces as they analyzed what they might gain, he feared that explaining to them wouldn't solve anything. It hurt him to know that they only had taken him in for the money.

Mandy had lost trust in the world. Had Maria and Andrew confronted him without him knowing what they already knew, he would have told them the truth and counted on them to keep his secret. But knowing what he did now, he feared that if they found out they couldn't get any money from him, they might betray him and lure him into the trap of his enemies.

Just like the Malian proverb said, a deaf man does not need to hear the drums of war before he flees from the path of danger. Mandy didn't need a soothsayer to tell him that his days of relative comfort were over. Later that night, when the couple had gone into their room, Mandy drew out his bag from under the bed and picked up his documents. Sadness filled his soul as he flipped through the pages. Those papers were supposed to keep him safe in foster care for at least nine months, more if his foster parents had good things to report about him, but if he stepped out of that door and walked into the streets, he would become an illegal immigrant. At least until he turned eighteen, his visa was dependent upon him staying with his foster family. He slid down from the bed onto the floor and picked up a thick winter jacket, his notepads, story manuscripts, and his blanket. He stuffed them all into his backpack and opened the door. He peered into the hallway; it was clear. As he walked toward the living room, where the sound of the television was still high, he could hear Maria giggling from inside their room. He passed through the living room, opened the door slightly, and walked away, never to return.

Chapter Twenty-One

The cold of the night hit Mandy as he left the brick building that had been his home for the past five months. He wore the thick jacket over his shirt and looked left and right at the empty street, wondering where to go from here.

He could see a few cars driving past on the main road at the end of the street. He knew it was dangerous to walk in the streets at this hour; he had heard stories of people who were robbed on their way back from the clubs in the wee hours of the night. He had also seen, some weeks ago on his way to school, policemen gathered around a convenience store roped off with yellow-and-black tape. Gloved officers were picking up items and snapping pictures of the broken glass windows like they did in the crime shows he watched. It was later reported on the news that armed robbers had broken into the store at night and killed one of the employees who had been sleeping inside the store, hoping to save enough money to rent an apartment.

Mandy walked faster as he passed the storefront and didn't look back until he was on the deserted main road. The street was well-lit with streetlamps and the neon signs that lined both sides. He could hear the sirens of police cars blaring away in the distance, putting a dent in the deafening silence of the night.

He wished he could run toward the sirens, to keep himself safe with the police all through the night, but he couldn't risk being taken back to his foster home, or worse, deported back to Mali. Mandy kept close to the shuttered storefronts to hide himself in the shadows of the buildings. From time to time, he would see the headlights of a car driving down the street. He would quicken his steps and hide between two buildings until the car zoomed past.

He got to an intersection and heard some voices under a dark bridge in front of him. He ran and hid behind a truck parked by the side of the road and observed as some people walked up and down under the bridge. He feared that they might be armed robbers, preparing to go and rob another business, or maybe they had just finished a robbery and had stopped to share their loot.

He looked around and saw a man lying on some raised pavement beside one of the pillars of the bridge. There were a few other people nearby, some sitting, others lying down. He could hear them talking and laughing without any fear of the darkness. Mandy walked down to the bridge, and as soon as the people there saw him, they quieted and stared at him like he was an alien.

There were men, boys of his age and younger, and one woman who looked so masculine that Mandy could have sworn she was a man if not for her tiny singsong voice when she broke the silence and asked, "Hey, you, boy! Whatcha looking at? Why you stare at me like that?"

Mandy's eyes opened wide as the woman walked angrily toward him.

"Whatcha want? Huh? What are you staring at? You wanna come try your shit with me tonight? Bring it on!"

She pushed Mandy. He staggered backward and stepped on a man sleeping on the ground next to him.

"What the fuck!" the man cursed and stood up. He towered above Mandy. Even in the near darkness of the night under the bridge, Mandy could see the man's angry eyes—two big bloodshot eyes popping out of a shining bald head.

"Are you blind or something?" the man asked, looking down at him.

Mandy gripped tightly onto the straps of his backpack, but still his hands quivered. He could hear his heart pounding in his chest, and his bladder threatened to release its contents down his leg.

"Come on, man. Chill out," another man said, standing up. "He's just a kid." He patted the angry man on the shoulder to calm him down.

"Damn!" the angry man shouted. "I was this close." He pressed his thumb and index finger together. "I mean, this close to winning fifty mil in the lottery, and this fella had to wake me up."

The others laughed. "Get right back to the dream, bro! Go get that moolah!" a voice shouted, and the laughter continued.

The man who calmed the angry man down took Mandy's hand and led him toward his mat.

"Where you taking the boy to? I was just kidding. I wanna be friends too," the woman said jokingly.

"Keep tripping, Jessie. It's your thing," the man said dismissively, and pointed at his mat. "Sit," he said. Then he hushed his voice. "What are you doing out here in the night? Don't you know it's dangerous?"

Mandy told the man that he was just looking for somewhere to sleep. He lied that he had just been kicked out by his friend who he was squatting with, so he had no place to go.

The man allowed him to share his mat. Mandy opened his backpack and brought out the blanket. He wrapped himself up with it and used the backpack as a pillow. His breath was measured, and his eyes darted around and around. He feared something dangerous might happen. The choking smell of Indian hemp hung so heavy in the air that he could feel his lungs shrink as it hit them. He felt the urge to cough, but he did not want to draw any more attention to himself, so he covered his face with the blanket and shut his eyes tight.

He said a little prayer for himself and Hamza. "Dear God, if you really exist up there, please keep my little brother safe. Shield him in the rainy days, wrap heavy woolen blankets around him on cold days, and never let his mouth lack a meal to eat. Keep him in your way, and never let him lose himself in this cruel world."

* * *

The next morning the loud sound of car horns woke him. He pulled the blanket off his face and saw that the underpass, which had been crowded with homeless people overnight, was now deserted. The mat was gone, and he was lying on the ground. He got up, dusted himself off, and folded the blanket into his backpack.

"I didn't bring my toothbrush," he sighed. But even if he had brought the toothbrush along, he wasn't sure of getting toothpaste or water to wash his mouth.

Mandy walked around the streets of the Bronx, not knowing exactly where to go. He was hungry, his legs were weak, and he still felt chills in his spine after sleeping on that cold sidewalk. He knew Maria and Andrew would be looking for him now. They must have woken up and gone to his room after rehearsing their lines about what to tell him to make him hand over the money they hoped he had. It would dawn on them that he must have overheard their conversation the previous night.

The cold street was rowdy with the late-morning rush. Two things were at the forefront of Mandy's mind. First, he wanted to get as far away from Andrew and

Maria as he could. Second, he needed to get something to eat. He had decided to go to Brooklyn, where they wouldn't think he'd be, but he couldn't trek that distance on an empty stomach.

At the end of a street off Westchester Avenue, he saw some construction workers. The street had been closed with wooden barricades, and triangular street signs advertised "Men at Work." A slim Chinese man wearing a straw hat yelled instructions at an African American man sitting behind the steering wheel of a backhoe, one of many construction vehicles working on the street.

Mandy stood and observed for a while, and then he approached the Chinese man. "Good morning, sir," he said.

The man turned and looked at him. "Yes? Yes? Why are you coming to work by this time? It's almost ten!" the man barked.

Mandy looked around, just to be sure the man was talking to him.

"I'm talking to you!" the Chinese man snapped impatiently. "You are fired!"

"Sir, I am sorry. I came to look for a job. I don't work here yet," Mandy said in a calm voice.

The man looked around to check on his workers. "Hey, you! Stop standing around. Where are the sprayers?" One of the guys in a blue jumpsuit and heavy black shoes hurried off. The backhoe driver was busy digging the sharp end of the loader into a heap of concrete.

"You say you want to work?" the man said to Mandy.

"Yes."

The man looked him over from head to toe, pulled a pack of cigarettes and lighter from his pocket, and brought one out. He put the cigarette between his lips and pressed the lighter. He covered the tiny tongue of fire on the lighter with a cupped palm and lit his cigarette. He inhaled deeply and sent rings of smoke circling up toward the skies. Then he looked at Mandy and said with a wave of his hand, "You don't look strong."

Mandy pleaded with the man. He begged him to give him a chance, that he was stronger than he looked. The man was a hard nut to crack, but Mandy would not back down.

"Okay, you can work today," the man said finally.

Happy that he had found a way of making some money, Mandy dropped his bag and started unzipping his jacket. But the Chinese man still seemed uneasy about his decision. "Do you have a work permit? Let me see your papers," he said.

Mandy's heart froze for a second. He stuttered as the Chinese man stretched forth his hand. "I don't have a permit," he stammered.

"Oh, I see..." the man said, giving Mandy a wan smile. "Give me a moment. I'll be back." He walked toward a small truck parked at the construction site.

"Hey!" the African American man yelled.

Mandy saw the man waving him away.

"Go! Go!" the man said in a loud whisper. Mandy drew closer. "Go now," the man said. "He's going to call immigration."

Like a bullet shot out of a gun, Mandy grabbed his backpack and started running. He ran even faster than he had when the armed mob attacked them on their way to Tangier. Though people stared at him suspiciously, Mandy did not stop running until he reached a deserted alley around East 177th Street. He leaned on the wall for a while to catch his breath, then continued his long walk to downtown Brooklyn.

Chapter Twenty-Two

Early that same afternoon, Mandy lost the ability to feel. Trekking around the busy streets of Brooklyn, he thought of throwing himself in front of one of the cars driving by to end his life and all of the suffering it brought. Although he had not eaten anything all day, he no longer felt the biting pain in his lower abdomen. He couldn't feel his legs. His eyelids were too tired to stay open, so they just hung limp as he walked like a drunk man, staggering along aimlessly.

A passerby's shoulder hit his own, and he fell to the ground.

"Oh, I'm sorry," a young woman said as she bent down and offered Mandy her hand, helping him to his feet. "Are you okay?"

Mandy slowly slipped his hand out of hers. He felt very embarrassed, not because he fell, but because it was a woman who had knocked him down. He felt it was a disgrace and didn't speak well of him as a young man. He remembered what his mother always told Hamza: "A man is supposed to be strong. He is not supposed to cry or whimper like a little baby."

As he stood and started beating the dust off his bottom, he knew that he had just disgraced his mother.

He imagined her rolling in her grave. The thought made him consider what had happened to his parents' bodies. Would his Uncle Abdulsalaam hide them and bury them in a shallow grave, or would he give them the state burial royalty deserved? If he organized a state burial for them, what would he tell the people of Sikasso? What would he tell the kings and queens from other kingdoms who would attend the funeral?

"Are you okay?" the woman asked again, pulling Mandy away from his thoughts.

He nodded. He could feel his head swirling as he walked away.

The woman, a petite Latina, stood watching him as he staggered toward a wooden bench by the side of the road. She followed him and sat beside him on the bench.

"Are you all right? Do you want to see a doctor?"

"No, I'm fine. I'll be fine," Mandy snapped, still feeling embarrassed that he had been thrown down by the mere shoulders of a young woman who looked to be no more than nineteen.

She would, however, not let it go. She looked at him, from the dusty shoes on his legs to the beads of sweat on his forehead and sighed. She opened her black Chanel handbag, brought out a bag, and gave it to him.

"This is my lunch," she said with a smile, "but I think you need it more."

Mandy looked from her hand to her face; then he looked away. A big lump of shame filled his stomach, and like ice dropped inside boiling water, he felt the shame melting and dripping into every part of him. He hesitated, but she shoved the bag into his hand and placed her hand on his.

"We all have our low days," she whispered before she put her hand back into her bag and brought out a half-filled bottle of Pepsi.

"Sorry, but I already drank some," she said as she placed it on the bench. Then she walked away.

Mandy looked at the drink beside him and turned to look at the woman. She looked back at the same time, and their eyes met. He muttered, "Thank you," and although the woman couldn't hear him, she saw the movement of his lips and winked at him. His face flushed with embarrassment, and he looked away.

Clutching the lunch bag and drink closely to him, Mandy walked into a nearby park, which was busy with children running around, playing on the swings and merry-go-rounds, and parents hanging around or sitting on the benches and cheering them on.

Mandy went to the park office and asked if he could use the bathroom. Two ladies at the counter pointed him to the bathroom, and as soon as he was inside, he locked the door behind him and dropped his bag beside the sink. He turned on the tap and scooped some water into his mouth. He gargled with the water and spat it out, before he scooped in another palm full. He repeated this over and over; then he put his palm a few inches away from his mouth and blew some air into it to check his breath. He rinsed his mouth a little more, and then he washed his legs, head, face, hands, and armpits. He stood for a while, waiting to dry, before he pulled on his sweaty clothes, wishing he had brought a change or two.

He stood in front of the mirror and admired himself. He dug his fingers into his wet hair and ruffled it. It was fluffy, curly, and shiny. He smiled at himself. He may have lost everything, but he still had his charm, as verified when he stepped out and caught the two ladies at the counter staring at him. He nodded slightly, and one of them, a slim black girl, put a hand over her mouth and smiled sheepishly.

Mandy wandered farther into the park and found a bench. He started munching his food—a delicious cheeseburger with bacon. He dug his teeth into the burger and chewed like a hungry wolf that had finally found prey after weeks of unsuccessful hunting. As he swallowed the last piece and gulped down his Pepsi, someone sat down beside him and offered him a familiar smile.

"Hi," she said, stretching out her hand. Her voice was breezy.

"Hello," Mandy replied, wondering where he had seen that face before.

Instead of taking her hand, he showed her the grease on his own from the food he had just eaten. She lowered her hand. Mandy realized then that she was one of the ladies at the office counter.

"I'm Cassie," she said.

"I'm Mandy."

An awkward silence hung between them. Cassie was still smiling, but she looked uneasy, and her eyes darted back and forth. Mandy thought maybe she had just come to watch the children play, so he didn't say a word. He just sat there and savored the beautiful feeling of having food in his stomach after a long day's walk.

"You don't look like you have a kid," Cassie said after a long moment of silence.

"Me? Kid? How do you mean?"

"I mean, this is a park, and people come here with their kids. So...?" She shrugged; her smile radiant.

"Well, I don't have a kid," he said.

"Okay, so you just came to chill, yeah?" she continued.

Mandy wanted to ask her if she was the chief security guard, whose job was to question everyone at the park, but he knew what she was doing and decided to play along.

"Yeah, just chilling," he replied.

She looked questioningly at the backpack sitting beside him, and he wondered what she was thinking. Could she possibly think he was homeless? It seemed absurd, but he realized that was the actual truth. He was, in fact, a homeless guy wandering around the city.

"Okay," she said. She rocked slowly on the seat.

Without making it obvious, Mandy followed the movement of her eyes as she looked backward again. He saw a lady standing in front of the building, making hand gestures to her. When she noticed Mandy looking, she quickly brought down her hand and acted as if she was looking elsewhere.

Mandy smiled. Now he got it. The girl had something to say, but she didn't have the courage to say it.

"So where are you going from here? My shift is about to end. Do you want to hang out and eat lunch? We could go over to my place later and eat pancakes. I make very delicious pancakes, and it's just a short walk away," she said, smiling at him suggestively.

Mandy thought for a moment. He was not going to embarrass himself by taking a girl out when he knew he didn't have a dime on him. Although he knew some girls in the West did not mind splitting tabs, that wasn't for him. Mandy could use a timeout, time just to chat and forget everything that was going wrong in his life. But he just couldn't get himself to ask her if she planned to pay. For a man to allow a woman to pay the tab was a weak thing to do.

Even considering the possibility made Musa remember a girl whose boyfriend had embarrassed her at their hotel in Bamako. Musa had gone to spend some alone time there last summer to work on a school project. One evening, he had gone downstairs to chat with the staff, some of whom he was very fond of. When he got to the kitchen, he saw a strange man at the sink washing dishes. He greeted the man and asked the chef if they had hired a new employee, but the chef said no and went ahead to narrate the story.

The young man had come to the restaurant with his girlfriend. After they had eaten, the man checked his front pocket but couldn't find his wallet. He ransacked all of his pockets but still couldn't find it. His girlfriend, out of embarrassment, asked how much the bill was. When they told her, she dug into her purse and counted out half of the bill. She said the half she was paying for was her own part, and then, to the astonishment of the boyfriend and everyone else at the restaurant, she walked away. Because he wasn't a regular customer and because there wasn't any other thing they could do, the manager asked the young man to go to the kitchen and wash dishes. He was to work for eight hours to cover his debt. Hearing the story, Musa had laughed heartily and then asked them to let the young man go.

Mandy wanted to accept Cassie's offer. She was a beautiful girl, the kind Mandy would like to hang out with, but how would he tell her that the backpack beside him was the only thing he had to his name?

"Love blinds," he reminded himself, "and although I'm already at my lowest point, it would be foolish to trust this stranger."

"I'm sorry, Cassie. I can't come with you. Maybe some other time. I need to catch up with some friends," he said. He stood and walked away, taking with him the image of her beautiful smile.

* * *

The nights brought more coldness and hunger—the bane of Mandy's new life. It had been two weeks since he had become homeless, and every passing day seemed to be worse than the one preceding it.

One night, he stood near a trash can behind a building, waiting for passersby to disperse so he could forage for leftover food. He had not been very lucky that day. It seemed like there was so much hunger in Brooklyn that no one had any leftovers.

He had only eaten three small cookies he had picked up from the ground when they fell from the hands of a little boy. Having seen the boy rocking up and down excitedly in his mother's arm as they walked down to the subway station, he'd followed them, thinking that the kid looked likely to drop the cookies. When he did, Mandy dashed toward them, glancing around quickly before he bent down and picked up the package. That was breakfast, and since then, he hadn't had anything else.

The men he had met on the stoop of the homeless shelter where he had been sleeping for the past two days had put immense fear into him with their stories of how the Immigration and Naturalization Service had deported a man back to Ghana the other day. They said the man's papers had expired eight months ago, and he had been successfully running from INS until his ex-girlfriend saw him on a train and alerted a policeman.

"I'm gonna miss Charley, man," one of the men said as he gulped down the last drop in his tiny whiskey bottle. He squeezed his face together as the heat hit his throat. Then he exhaled like a man who had been forced to swallow the extracts of bitter leaf, before he started talking about the other homeless people he'd known who had been deported back to Africa and the Middle East for not having their papers. Some of them had gone to look for a job, and the employer had called INS to arrest them.

Mandy was scared. He needed a job but looking for one wasn't even an option. He couldn't risk getting deported. The moment he stepped on Malian soil his grave would be an arm's length away.

Having had no luck with the trash cans, Mandy snuck into the premises of one of the biggest five-star hotels in the city. He hid under a tree, waiting for the hotel restaurant to close. The restaurant was in a detached bungalow, while the suites and guest rooms were in the main building. He had been here a few times to forage their dumpsters in the back, but the foods he found there were either almost spoiled or contaminated by the dirty surface of the dumpster. When he had managed to eat them, his stomach had ached terribly.

He had heard that the restaurant closed before midnight, so he decided to hang around and wait so he could try his luck inside the kitchen. He hoped he would find fresh leftovers to eat. Mandy patiently stood and watched as the guests left one after another. Then the lights inside the restaurant went off, and the last person came out. She turned the OPEN sign on the door around to CLOSED and walked away, holding her mobile phone to her ear.

Mandy stood there waiting for her to come back to lock the door, but she was so engrossed in the phone call that she didn't come back. This was his chance. His eyes darted left and right. Then he snuck in. First, he walked to the back of the bar. Wads of cash were lying on an open ledger book. His heart skipped a beat as he stared at the money.

"How could these people be this careless?" he wondered as he scanned for anything edible. He only found bottles of wine. He looked at the wads of money again and imagined how much it was. His heart raced at the thought that this money could solve some of his most pressing problems. He contemplated picking it up, but as soon as the thought came to his mind, he felt disgusted. "God forbid!" he cursed under his breath. He left the money and walked through a passageway into the kitchen. The kitchen smelled heavenly.

"Finally, the smell of good food!" he sighed. He opened the long ash-colored fridge by the entrance and gasped at the plenty within. It brought back a known feeling—the feeling of home! In the upper compartment were stacks of meat; in the middle were transparent plastic containers of leftover Chinese fried rice. By the door were bottles of fruit juice, oranges, and slices of bread wrapped in plastic bags.

Mandy took a bottle of juice and a bag of bread. He tore the package open and started to devour the bread like a hungry lion. Then he picked up a plastic plate from the kitchen counter and started to scoop some rice onto it. After scooping the rice, he placed the container back in the fridge. As he closed the fridge, he saw a pudgy old man standing at the door of the kitchen holding a long plank.

Mandy reached for the plate immediately, ready to grab it and run away.

"If you move, I'll smash your head!" the old man threatened.

Mandy put the plate down. "I am sorry, sir. I am very sorry. I only came to look for food." He dropped to his knees and started pleading.

"Liar! You're a thief. Try anything funny and I'll kill you right here before the cops arrive," the man barked. He brought out a phone from his pocket and began to dial 911.

"Please, sir, please don't do this," Mandy pleaded. Tears flooded his face. "I am not a thief. I only came to look for food to eat. You can check at the bar. I saw some wads of cash there. I didn't even touch it. I swear, I didn't touch it. It's still there. It's just food that I want."

At that moment, a female voice spoke from the phone, "Hello, this is 911. What's your emergency?"

"Please, sir, please." Mandy lowered his voice, pressed his hands together like he was praying, and lowered himself.

The man kept quiet and observed him, his eyes sweeping across Mandy's body from head to toe, as if trying to figure out if he was armed.

"Hello? Are you there?" the voice on the phone asked. "It's okay if you can't say anything, but please stay on the line so we can trace your location. Help is on the way."

"Hey, don't worry. This call was a mistake. Sorry," the old man said, and ended the call.

The man dropped the phone on the counter, lowered the plank, and asked Mandy to stand. "What's your name? And what do you have on that plate?" he asked.

"My name is Mandy. It's Chinese rice," Mandy said. "I'll put it back. Thanks for not reporting me." He went to the fridge to put back the food, but the old man stopped him. He grabbed the plate, put it in the microwave, and pointed at the table in the center of the room. Mandy went and sat down, and the man followed with the warmed plate of rice.

"Tell me about yourself," the old man said. "You speak so well. How did you end up on the streets?"

Chapter Twenty-Three

"I came to the U.S. to seek a better life," Mandy began. "Assassins invaded our house some months ago and killed my parents, but my little brother and I were lucky to escape. Life became so difficult after that tragedy, and we were scared that the assassins would come back to attack us, so we went on the run until we finally decided to take the ultimate risk. We boarded one of those migrant boats that smuggle people to Europe." He paused and shut his eyes tightly to force back the tears forming under his eyelids.

The old man, who said his name was Mr. Kojo, shook his head compassionately and tapped his hand on Mandy's.

"They separated me and my brother in Spain, and right now, I don't really know where he is. My foster parents suddenly became hostile to me, and I overheard them planning to have me deported if I didn't give them some of the money they think my parents left me."

"Wow." The old man was surprised. His voice was deep and coarse. He picked his words slowly and carefully, as if it took him great effort to speak. "Did they really plan to take advantage of you despite what you've been through?"

Mandy shrugged. "The sad thing is that I don't have access to any money. I knew they wouldn't believe me, so I had to walk away. That's how I got here. I was dying of hunger until I found this place. I am sorry. I've never stolen before in my life." Mandy edged toward his knees again, but the old man held him back.

"It's okay. I understand. The fact that you didn't take that money is proof that you are sincere."

A feeling of guilt washed over Mandy. He felt bad that he hadn't told the man the entire truth about his life story. For a moment, he contemplated whether he should just come clean and tell him everything, but it was already too late. Admitting that he had told a half-truth may damage what little faith the old man had in him.

The old man did not take his eyes off Mandy, even as the man's eyes became cloudy with tears.

"Are you okay, sir?" Mandy asked, feeling awkward that the man was crying because of him.

Mr. Kojo blinked repeatedly. He then offered to give Mandy shelter in his home and a job in the restaurant. Mr. Kojo was the manager of the hotel, but since Mandy didn't have the legal requirements to be properly employed, the old man said he'd have to work off the record, and he would pay him from his personal salary so there wouldn't be anything to cause suspicion during internal auditing. Later that night, on the drive to Mr. Kojo's house, the old man explained that Mandy reminded him so much of his son who had died two years earlier, and that was why he couldn't hold back his tears.

* * *

Mandy stood in front of the large mirror in the staff common room and admired himself. The blue-and-white housekeeping uniform looked so good on him. The white short-sleeve shirt clung to his body, highlighting his robust chest and perfectly toned abs. The immaculate white color of the shirt perfectly complemented the olive-black color of his skin. He had spent so much time ironing the shirt that the edges looked razor-sharp, like it could cut the finger of anyone who tried to touch it. His smile was radiant and had not left his face since Mr. Kojo told him that he could work at the hotel. Mr. Kojo was heaven-sent, and all Mandy wanted to do was impress him.

"Hey, everyone, hurry up!" Franklin, the housekeeping coordinator, said as he entered the common room. Everyone finished their dressing and checked off their names on the roster on the counter.

"Hey, Mandy, work with Annie today. She'll teach you everything you need to know," Franklin said, and Annie, a slim girl with long blonde hair tied into a ponytail, walked up to Mandy.

Annie's voice sounded airy when she said hi, and then she flashed a beautiful smile that lasted only a second. She picked up some bed sheets from the table in the center of the room and heaped them on her arm. Then she asked Mandy to get the rest and follow her.

As they walked through the glossy marble of the hallway to the rooms designated to them, Mandy noticed the practiced way Annie swung her slender waist. At the first room, she made him watch while she made the bed. After she had made the beds in three different suites, she asked him to make the fourth one. She leaned against the door of the room with her hands folded, watching him. After he made the bed, she clapped for him.

"Bravo," she said. "I guess your girlfriend doesn't have to make the bed before and after." She laughed.

Mandy managed a smile. Then he picked up the old bedspreads to drop them outside the door, from where the laundrymen would pick them up immediately.

Annie, however, refused to let him pass. "Hey, you didn't answer the question?" she said.

"What question?" he asked, feigning ignorance.

"Does she make the bed before and after, or do you do it?"

Mandy laughed. "Is that your way of asking if I have a girlfriend? Well, I don't have one. Now can we hurry up? We still have five more rooms to go."

Throughout the day, Annie flirted with him. She said she could not believe that someone as handsome as he was could be without a girlfriend. At the end of the morning shift, she asked if he would like to have lunch with her, but although Mandy liked her friendly nature and wouldn't mind being friends with her, he felt it was too early to start getting too close to people, especially co-workers. Besides, he needed to keep as much of a low profile as he could, so he lied that he needed to run some errands for Mr. Kojo.

Mandy lived in one of the rooms in Mr. Kojo's three-bed-room bungalow. Mr. Kojo looked like he was in his early sixties. Before Mandy came, Mr. Kojo lived alone, but he had a cook and a cleaner who came around every day. On the wall of the large living room were pictures of him with his daughter, Bridget, who was busy at Columbia University studying for her master's degree. Mr. Kojo said his ex-wife left him about fifteen years ago, eloping with a younger lover and leaving him to raise their daughter and late son alone.

With a cook and a cleaner in the house, Mandy had no chores to do after work. For the first time in a long time, he had people cleaning up after him. However, this time, it felt awkward, and he refused to let himself get used to it. Instead he would wake early in the morning and clean some part of the house before the cleaner showed up. Mr. Kojo would always chastise him, but Mandy would lie that he just wasn't used to having someone do house-work for him and that it made him feel too docile.

Mandy worked in the housekeeping department for three weeks before he was promoted to waiter. The supervisors were pleased with how fast he learned and his enthusiasm, and they were impressed by the number of guests who specifically requested that he be the one to come to their rooms whenever they needed anything. Mr. Kojo paid him in cash at the end of every week, and once he had saved enough money, he bought a phone, eager to resume his search for Hamza.

Chapter Twenty-Four

The day Mandy got his cell phone, he sent an email to the Spanish immigration office requesting the details of the family that fostered Desmond Collins, the name he had seen written on Hamza's papers. In the email, he claimed that he, Mandy Patrick, had gotten his legal papers and was hoping to reunite with his brother after almost a year of being apart.

After some days, the Spanish immigration office replied. They said they would search their records, but he would have to be patient, as there had been hundreds of thousands of underage immigrants at that time. Day after day Mandy waited, repeatedly checking his phone for emails or missed calls, but he heard nothing. He was desperate and scared. He needed answers. He needed to see his brother and be sure that he was alive and fine.

One afternoon after Mandy's morning shift, Mr. Kojo's driver drove Mandy back home. It had been four months since Mandy had started living with the man and working at the restaurant, but Mr. Kojo was careful not to let him go anywhere alone. The old man was wary of Mandy being caught by immigration officers, so he made sure that either he or his driver was with Mandy everywhere he went.

Mandy slid the glass door open and entered the marble-tiled living room, his shoes slapping the floor as he walked across it. A man dressed in a crisp white lab coat bent over the sofa. As Mandy drew closer, he saw that the man had a stethoscope plugged into his ears and pressed against Mr. Kojo's chest. Mandy's heart missed a beat as he wondered what was wrong with the old man.

"Are you alright?" he asked, taking a seat beside Mr. Kojo on the couch.

The old man nodded. The doctor removed the stethoscope, scribbled some words on his paper pad, and started wrapping the cuff of his blood pressure monitor around the old man's arm. Mandy watched with heightened interest as the doctor completed checking the old man's blood pressure and made another note on his paper pad.

"Nurse Susan will send your new pills later this evening," the doctor said as he packed his equipment into his black bag lying on the other sofa. He asked Mr. Kojo to rest more often, and then he shook hands with the man and Mandy before he left.

"I didn't know you were ill," Mandy said as soon as they were alone.

"Oh, come on," the old man scoffed. "It's just routine medical care. I'm in my mid-sixties, so some joints are getting cranky." Mr. Kojo tried to wave the topic away jokingly, but Mandy wasn't convinced.

"Are you sure you'll be alright?" he pressed on.

Shadows of Exile

"I am alright, Mandy," said Mr. Kojo, refusing to talk about it any further. "Anything from the Spaniards yet?"

Mandy exhaled. "Not yet. I sent them another email yesterday to remind them of their promise. I hope they respond this time."

"I hope so too. Anyway, I've got good news!" Mr. Kojo announced, rubbing his hands gleefully. "Bridget called. She'll be visiting in a month's time."

"Oh wow! That's great!" Mandy had never seen the old man this happy before. The smile on his face was radiant. It seemed like ten years had been wiped away. Mandy was happy for him, but as he walked down the hallway to his room, mixed feelings engulfed him. He was unsure of how to feel about having another person in the house. Although it was Mr. Kojo's daughter, he was wary that she may not be as welcoming as her father had been. Worse still, he was nervous about someone else knowing his story. The experience with Maria had taught him a bitter lesson that he couldn't trust people easily, no matter how nice they may seem at first. As he changed into his house clothes, Mandy decided it was high time he got a small apartment and moved out. He knew Mr. Kojo wouldn't be happy about this, but he had to do it.

* * *

Dressed in his crisp white uniform, Mandy finished serving a couple and was walking back toward the kitchen when a man walked into the restaurant with what appeared to be his wife and daughter. Mandy went to the menu stand and picked up three menus.

"Good afternoon and welcome to Gourmet DeStefano," he said. "Here's your menu. I'm at your service." He bowed slightly.

The woman and her daughter picked up their menus, while the husband, a heavyset, bald man, looked at the name tag on his shirt and smiled. "Mandy, it seems like you're new here."

"Oh yes, I'm quite new. Just about three months, but I can serve you just as perfectly as you've always been served here."

"I see." The man looked at his daughter, who was staring past the name tag on Mandy's shirt to appreciate his bulging chest. "Sweetheart, have you made a choice?"

The girl cleared her throat and turned back to the menu, trying to decide. "You see," the man continued, "she just graduated from college, so we are celebrating."

"Wow, congratulations, miss," Mandy said, and bowed again.

"Cheryl," the girl stated, extending her hand.

"Hi, Cheryl. Congratulations." Mandy shook her hand.

"Thanks, Mandy." She blushed.

Mandy noticed that Cheryl's mom had a rather stern look on her face. She quickly placed her order, and as Mandy wrote it down on his notepad, she glared at Cheryl, who couldn't take her eyes off of Mandy's body.

When Mandy brought their order, he found Mr. Kojo standing beside the man, talking and smiling. As he served their food, he caught Cheryl staring again. He had gotten used to female guests staring at him, but Cheryl had caught his attention, and he couldn't help but stare back.

Later in the kitchen, Mandy learned that Cheryl's father was Mr. Hugo, the owner of the hotel. They said that apart from Gourmet DeStefano, he also owned seven other five-star hotels in Brooklyn and Queens and a wine bar in Washington, DC. That day, the staff worked twice as hard. Everyone was proactive, getting the orders ready and serving the guests more quickly than they did on other days.

As Mandy served his other guests, he would look over at Mr. Hugo's table and find Cheryl still staring at him. He didn't smile the way he did earlier. The last thing he needed in his life right now was to lose this job, and he feared that flirting with the boss's daughter would be the easiest way to do that. Mandy felt his heart miss a beat when Cheryl and her parents stood to leave. The doormen opened the door; Cheryl and her mother left first, while Mr. Hugo followed closely with the assistant manager, Alex Boaz, who was talking to the boss and smiling like a sales-rep lobbying for a contract.

Mandy did not like Mr. Boaz, and he wasn't the only one. Some said he always overdid everything; others said he was a social climber. They said he used to work with them in the kitchen, but he somehow had managed to work his way into Mr. Hugo's good graces. Some said he took advantage of Mr. Hugo's cheerful nature, while others said he was promoted to assistant manager because he always rushed to give Mr. Hugo reports of everything happening in the restaurant.

Chapter Twenty-Five

C heryl was lying in bed flipping through the pages of a fashion magazine when someone knocked on the door.

"Yeah, come in," she responded, her eyes glued to the pictures of the models.

The door opened, and Samantha entered. "Hey, babes, hope I didn't take too long," Samantha said as she dropped her bag on the bed, sat down, and pulled off her shoes. "Damn! My feet are killing me!" she whined.

"Nah...you didn't take too long. Tell me, what do you think about this dress?" Cheryl sat up and pointed at a dress she liked.

Samantha was Cheryl's closest friend. They had become friends in high school, but unlike Cheryl, Samantha hadn't had the opportunity to go to college. During their sophomore year in high school, Samantha's dad died in Syria during a peacekeeping mission. Cheryl and Samantha had just become friends when Samantha's father died. The death dealt a heavy blow to Samantha that turned her into a shadow of herself. She was no longer the fun-loving girl who taught other cheerleaders new dance steps each time the school basketball team had a game. Instead, she stayed away from school, and the days she managed to come, she isolated herself from others, drowning in the pool of sadness that her life had become.

Cheryl provided a shoulder for her to cry on. She was always with her in school, and Samantha sometimes went over to Cheryl's house for a sleepover. They became inseparable, and when Cheryl was to about to leave for college, she helped Samantha get a job in her father's restaurant.

"I think the slit is too high," Samantha said, looking at the dress.

"Well maybe I'll tell the designer not to make it so high." Cheryl turned the page to show Samantha some other designs, then remembered she had a question for Samantha. "Hey! Who's that cute new guy at the restaurant?"

"Which guy?" Samantha rolled her eyes.

"Mandy."

"Oh, he's not totally new. He's been around for about three or four months," Samantha answered, continuing to check out the pictures.

Cheryl expected more. "Okay?"

"Okay what?" Samantha seemed surprised. "What about him?"

"Just anything. He's so cute, and I love the way he looked at me the other day." Cheryl blushed.

"Wow! He was checking you out?" Samantha laughed.

"Yeah?" Cheryl looked at her suspiciously. There was something condescending about Samantha's laughter that made Cheryl feel uneasy. "What's wrong with him checking me out?"

"Nothing. I am just surprised because he acts like he doesn't have time for girls."

"Oh, I see," Cheryl said playfully. "So, you've been hitting on him, and he hasn't been giving you the green light?"

"Hell no!"

They both started laughing.

* * *

One evening at the restaurant, Mandy had just finished clearing a table after a couple finished eating. As he dropped the dishes in the kitchen and came back into the restaurant, the doorman opened the door, and Cheryl entered. She looked beautiful in tight denim trousers that clung tightly to her thick hips, showing off her curvaceous body. She wore a milky white chiffon top, which accentuated her beautiful white skin and long honey-brown hair. She took off her dark shades and smiled at the doorman, and then one of the waiters, Mike, greeted her heartily and pointed her to a table just beside the window at the end of the large restaurant.

Mandy stood at a spot close to the kitchen door watching her as she took her seat. Her beauty was stunning, and Mandy wished he could walk up to her and tell her she was the most beautiful person he had seen today. His heart drummed thunderously in his chest, and he felt sweat spreading over his palms. He knew he wanted her, and for a fading moment, he remembered how perfect his life had once been. If things hadn't turned out the way they did, he would have had the courage to express the way he felt.

He wondered what her love life was like. Maybe she had a boyfriend or a fiancé from another wealthy family just like hers. Her boyfriend must be so refined and princely; she wouldn't want anything to do with someone like Mandy. As these thoughts rushed through his mind, Mandy remembered the way she had smiled at him the first time they met, and he hated himself for thinking she was trying to flirt with him. Maybe she was just being courteous and he had read it all wrong.

As Mandy was still standing there beating himself up, Mike tapped him on the shoulder. "She wants you to serve her. Here's her order." Mike shoved an order note into his hand.

"Who? What is...?" Mandy stammered, looking at the note.

"Miss Cheryl. She said I should ask you to bring her order," Mike explained, and then walked past Mandy.

Mandy walked into the kitchen, looking at the paper with disbelief. As soon as her order was up—a chicken sandwich and fresh pineapple juice—Mandy grabbed it and headed toward Cheryl's table. He wore a radiant smile as he approached the table.

"Good evening, Miss Cheryl," he greeted her.

"You can call me Cheryl, Mandy," she replied, giving him a bright smile.

"Okay, Cheryl. Here's your order." He bowed slightly and turned to leave.

"Umm...Mandy?" He turned back toward her. She looked him in the eyes. "Please sit with me for a moment," she said, after a brief pause during which she seemed to be debating whether to ask him or not.

"I...I," Mandy stammered.

"Please don't say 'no.'"

Mandy wanted to jump at the offer, but it seemed like this could be a trap.

"I am sorry. We have rules around here. I am sure you know." He declined, contrary to the desire of his heart.

"But I just want us to chat for a while. You're new here. I'd like to know you, and maybe be friends with you if you don't mind. I mean no harm."

"Okay, but the rules are—"

"Don't worry about the rules, Mandy. Come on, we can make an exception sometimes."

Looking around and feeling uneasy, Mandy pulled out a seat and sat down. He placed his tray on the table and looked at Cheryl, who had a naughty smile on her face.

"What?" he asked.

She laughed. "You know you just acted like a teenage girl being propositioned for the first time."

Mandy laughed. "You know I am just being careful, right?"

"Yeah, I know. I'm just messing with you." She picked up her sandwich and took a generous bite of it, and then she closed her eyes for a moment and savored the taste. "Mm, this is good," she gushed, and sipped her juice. She continued eating her food and watching Mandy, who was clearly very uneasy, without saying another word to him.

Mandy prayed that Mr. Kojo didn't come down from his office. He was about to take his leave, when Cheryl finally spoke.

"Why were you staring at me like that the other day?" Cheryl asked, an almost stern look on her face.

Mandy's eyes almost popped out of their sockets. "I wasn't."

"You were, Mandy. I saw you."

"No, not at all. I was just being courteous. Just like I am with every other customer. I'm sorry if I made you uncomfortable."

Cheryl laughed. She seemed to be enjoying the torture she was putting him through, and Mandy couldn't tell if she was being serious or playful. He chose to play it safe, to apologize for ever looking at her and then to try to avoid her table any other time she came to the restaurant. Once again, he felt stupid for thinking that this girl, as elegant and wealthy as she was, could feel even the slightest bit of attraction toward him.

Cheryl took a bite of her sandwich again and observed him for a moment. She looked in his eyes and held his gaze, but Mandy wouldn't let the flames of passion he thought he saw in those eyes fool him again. He averted his gaze and murmured that he'd like to get back to work.

"When is your shift ending?" she asked as he stood up.

"By six," he said reluctantly.

"Okay. Can I give you a ride? We need to finish this conversation."

Mandy wanted to tell her that they had nothing else to talk about, that he never wanted to see her again, that he wasn't comfortable with the mind game she was playing, but he couldn't say any of that, so he just nodded and walked away, escaping into the kitchen. He was both scared and angry. He was angry that, despite the obvious mind game she had just played with him, his heart still wanted to be close to her, but at the same time, he was scared he would get into trouble if this little fancy ever repeated itself. He was sure that Mr. Kojo wouldn't be happy to see him flirting with the boss's daughter, and he was even more certain that under the cheerful and friendly facade Mr. Hugo paraded around, there was a dangerous man who wouldn't spare anyone who tried to mess with the reputation of his family. He had seen

Mr. Hugo's type, and he was exactly the kind of person Mandy needed to avoid, at least until he figured out how to get himself legal status.

* * *

"Mandy! Mandy?" someone called in the common room. Mandy's shift had ended, and he was changing his clothes to go home. He turned and saw Samantha walking toward him.

"What's up?" he asked in a rather hostile manner. He wasn't in the mood for any girl to flirt with him.

She leaned back to observe his angry face. "Why you fuming?" she asked.

"What?" Mandy snapped again.

"Chill out, pretty boy. I ain't coming at you no more," she said. "I think Cheryl likes you." She stretched a paper toward him.

"What's that?" Mandy asked as he grabbed the paper from her and opened it.

"Uh huh! I know that look," she teased. "What does it say?"

She peeped at the paper, but Mandy quickly folded it up.

"Who's this from?" he asked.

"Cheryl. Mr. Hugo's daughter. So she's checking you out too? Hmm...Annie isn't gonna like this one bit."

"I told you I've got nothing with Annie."

"But she's got a lot with you," Samantha insisted, a teasing smile on her face. Just like Annie, Samantha had made passes at Mandy a few times, but he had turned her down politely yet managed to remain friends with her.

"So, Cheryl really gave you this?" he asked, trying to be sure that no one was playing with his emotions.

"Yeah, we're actually best friends," Samantha explained with a sense of pride, "and she asked about you a few days ago. I didn't know it was this serious. What are you guys up to?"

"Nothing, Samantha. We aren't even friends," he replied dismissively, putting the paper into his pocket.

Samantha got the hint that he didn't want to have that conversation. She just smiled, bragged that Cheryl would tell her anyways, and walked into the ladies' dressing room to get ready for her shift.

As soon as Samantha was out of sight, Mandy opened the note.

> *Okay, I know I made you feel uneasy, but that was exactly how your eyes made me feel even days after the first day we met. It was funny seeing you get all defensive. I mean, I enjoyed every moment of the taunt. Should I apologize? Maybe I should. That's why I'll be parked in front of Papa Joe's across the street, waiting for you to finish your shift. Be a gentleman and don't keep a girl waiting.*

Mandy smiled, and just like gasoline poured on a slab under the hot sun, the resentment that had built up in him in over the past two hours disappeared into thin air. He sent a text to Mr. Kojo's driver to tell him that he would hitch a ride with a friend, and then he left the building.

Mandy saw a white SUV and a black Toyota Camry parked in front of Papa Joe's pizza. He wondered which of the cars was Cheryl's. It would be odd to look inside both cars to check who the occupants were, but fortunately, just as he approached, the black Toyota drove off. However, he could now see that there was no one inside the white SUV. He frowned, wondering what to do, since he didn't have Cheryl's phone number. As he looked at his wristwatch to see if he had kept her waiting too long, he heard a sweet, tender voice call his name. He turned around and saw her coming out of the eatery holding a red pizza box.

"Did I keep you waiting too long?" he asked as he collected the box from her.

"No, you didn't," she said, flashing a smile. She unlocked the car, and they climbed in and drove off.

"So are you still mad at me?" she asked, winking at him.

"Umm...yeah, super mad," he teased, "but after reading your note, I don't know. I've been looking for that anger, but I can't find it."

She smiled and said she was sorry, that she was just trying to pull his leg. She turned on the stereo, and Usher's

"U Got It Bad" started playing. As they sang along, Cheryl went off-key each time she moved from the stanzas to the chorus, and then they'd both laugh, and Mandy would tease her, telling her what a terrible singer she was. They drove around for a while, talking about random things like movies, music, and food, until she finally dropped him off some blocks away from Mr. Kojo's house.

"Thanks for tonight, Mandy," she said as she turned off the car ignition.

"I should be the one thanking you. It's been a long time since I laughed so much in one day."

She smiled briefly. "Well, same here. It's been a very long time too."

Mandy didn't believe her, but he didn't argue. She already had a perfect life, so there was no way she could tell him truthfully that she didn't have happy moments every day. They stayed quiet for a moment, looking at each other and at the few cars passing. It seemed like she had something to say, but she wasn't forthcoming, so Mandy reached for the door and said goodnight.

"Can we do this again tomorrow?" she asked.

"Sure," Mandy blurted without giving it a thought. He told her he'd be on morning shift, so he'd be free at noon.

They said their goodbyes, and although Mandy wished that moment would never end, he exited the car and watched as she reversed and drove off before he walked the few blocks to Mr. Kojo's house.

* * *

Cheryl was ecstatic as she drove back home. Just as she had told Mandy, it had been a long time since she had had such a nice time. Her life would best be described as boring. Although she had everything other girls wished they had, she didn't have the happiness that comes with having warm people around her, especially the company of a guy she could be goofy with.

She heard her phone vibrating, and she reached for her bag in the back seat of the car. She unlocked the phone and saw that she had eleven missed calls from Edward. She was pissed. "Why would he call me eleven times?" She shoved the phone back into the bag and increased the volume of the car stereo.

As the gate of the Hugo mansion slid open and Cheryl drove up the well-lit driveway, she saw Edward's car leaving. The double-lane driveway had well-manicured lawns on both sides and a fresh-water fountain at the center, where the exit and entrance lanes converged. Cheryl turned off her headlights and remained in her spot, partly expecting that Edward would come around to ask why she hadn't been taking his calls, but mostly hoping he wouldn't notice her.

She was fuming. She was ready to shout at him and ask if he didn't have any honor to preserve. Didn't he think he deserved better than a woman who needed to be coerced into being with him? She was tired of playing along with this courtship, and tonight she was ready to shatter it like a vase against a concrete wall.

Cheryl gripped the steering wheel tightly, trying to summon the courage to say everything she wanted to say, but when Edward's car got to the gate, it didn't turn back around. The gate slid open as it sensed the car, and he drove off.

Cheryl's mom, Beatrice, was sitting in the living room when she walked into the house. "You just missed Edward by a few minutes. He was here to look for you. He said you weren't picking up his calls," her mother said, looking up from her phone.

"I saw him leaving, Mom," Cheryl replied and started up the stairs.

"So, did you talk?" Her mom's eyes brightened with expectation.

"We have nothing to talk about, Mom." Cheryl hastened her footsteps and hurried to her room to avoid the overbearing marriage lecture that came every time they talked about Edward. Running away may have worked for her other times, but it didn't save her this time. Her mom came knocking on her door a few minutes later.

"I think you should give yourself time to get to know him, Cheryl," her mom started as they both sat down on her bed.

"But, Mom, I've tried. I know him, but the feelings just aren't there."

"That's because you're not giving them a chance to sprout. Edward is a very nice young man, but you haven't let yourself accept this because we're the ones recommending him."

"But why can't I just choose my own man? Why can't I fall in love naturally like other girls and get married to the man I love?" she cried.

Her mom held her hand and patted it slowly. "You're not other girls, Cheryl. You're different. You can't just marry anybody. You have to consider your family. People marry for different reasons—for wealth, for power, for connections, to create opportunities, and unite empires. Love happens along the line during marriage for some; while others create it themselves before the wedding day. Only the poor marry simply because of love, and that's why they remain poor."

Her mom went ahead with the story Cheryl had heard over a thousand times, of how her father, Cheryl's grandfather, who used to own a chain of restaurants, was having a tough time in business and needed a loan to settle his debts. When he couldn't access a loan, he approached his old friend, Mr. Hugo's dad, who was in the same line of business, and they formed a merger. While Hugo's dad pumped more capital into the business, Beatrice's father, who was an excellent chef, created delicacies that made the whole city flood into their restaurants, forcing them to open several other outlets. To solidify this relationship, the two men matched up their children, Hugo and Beatrice, and after they got married, they continued the legacy, which had so far given birth to DeStefano and other five-star hotels and restaurants. This time around, Mr. Hugo wanted to run for governor, and being in-laws with the Senate majority leader, Senator Parker, was his best bet to become the Republican Party's flag bearer.

Chapter Twenty-Six

Mandy and Cheryl hung out almost every evening for two weeks. They visited local eateries, trying out taquerias, bistros, and African restaurants alike. Mandy made Cheryl do some things she hadn't done before, like trying out some African delicacies, taking long walks instead of going for a drive, and taking the public bus to the park on days she didn't want her parents to know she wasn't in her room. She would leave her car in the garage, take a taxi, and then ride around on the bus with Mandy.

With Mandy, life was an adventure. Unlike Edward, who was boring, rigid, and could only talk about work and politics, Mandy was versatile. He was too intelligent to be a waiter, but he still went about the job with his head held high. Cheryl felt safe around Mandy. Around him, she could be herself, she could try out silly things without fear of being judged. She could express her fears and talk about everything. Mandy became her best friend, and with time, she found herself telling him about the guys she had been with in college. She told him about all of her escapades—from the childish ones who didn't know how to treat a woman to the ones who bragged so much about their sexual prowess but ended up going only ten strokes before collapsing onto the bed. Yet she never brought up Edward because, although he hadn't said it yet, she knew that Mandy was in love with her as much as she was with him, and she didn't want to hurt him or make him feel insecure.

* * *

Mr. Kojo was not happy when Mandy said he was leaving. He asked him to stay, but Mandy's mind was already made up. He explained that he wanted to learn how to take care of himself, how to be a man, and not have everything already provided for him.

Mr. Kojo had reached out to some of his friends earlier to look for a way to secure legal residence and a work permit for Mandy, but they said that because Mandy had already been in the U.S. illegally for months, the only viable way to get him a green card would be for him to leave the U.S. for some time and then apply for a visa from another country. Then they could fast-track the process.

This arrangement didn't sit well with Mandy. If he tried to fly, the immigration officers would likely find out that he had been in the country without any legal papers, and then they might arrest him and deport him back to Mali. The only other option would be to smuggle himself out on a cargo ship, but that risk was not one he was willing to take, especially since he still hadn't reunited with his brother.

When Mr. Kojo remained opposed to Mandy moving out, Mandy explained that he just wanted to give the old man and his daughter space to spend some time alone, that he would visit while she was around, and he would return after she had gone back to Columbia University. After much talk, Mr. Kojo agreed, and Mandy went to live with his coworker Raheem in a small studio apartment on the outskirts of the city.

Mandy could not deny the way he felt about Cheryl. He dreamt of her every night, and thoughts of her were always the first thing that came to his mind when he woke. He had managed to keep his true identity away from her for many weeks. Just like in the movies, where a prince would disguise himself as a commoner and travel to a foreign land to look for love—someone who would love him for who he was and not for his status—Mandy was glad he had found someone who loved and wanted to be with him even while he was only a poor waiter. If only his life were truly like a movie and he could leave behind the nightmare elements and build a relationship with Cheryl that would last a lifetime.

* * *

One night, Mandy and Cheryl saw a stage play at a theatre. The play was about an African couple who eloped when the cruel king of their village wanted to take the bride away from the groom who was a slave from another village, which the kingdom had defeated in war many years before. The bride, who was one of the finest maidens in the land, had fallen in love with this slave, despite the king wanting her as his fifth wife.

A line spoken by an old woman in the play stuck in Cheryl's heart. She said, "When you're in love, don't waste a moment wondering if the feeling is right or wrong. Tomorrow is not assured, so make every moment of today count."

As Mandy and Cheryl walked toward the main road where they'd get a taxi for her, Cheryl noticed a small garden by the side of the street. She stopped and grabbed Mandy's hand.

"This place looks so beautiful," she said, dragging him into the garden.

The garden was dimly lit. The atmosphere was serene, with the smell of rosemary and lavender perfuming the air. Mandy and Cheryl stood there for a moment, admiring the beautiful flowers, and then when Cheryl turned to look at Mandy, her eyes met his, and she saw an undeniable passion in them. She froze for a moment, and then she drew him closer, pressed her lips against his, and they kissed as if tomorrow would never come.

"I love you, Mandy," she murmured into his mouth. He continued kissing her. His fingers mussed her hair, while his other hand pressed her waist firmly against his bulging crotch.

After they broke the kiss, Mandy moved away from her. "I love you too, Cheryl. I really love you. But you know this isn't right."

"Why? Why isn't it right? I love you, and I want us to be together."

Her fingers brushed against his, and he flinched, but as she tried to remove her hand, his fingers found hers, and they locked together.

Mandy swallowed hard. He felt jealousy filling his chest. "I learned you have a man. What, then, do you want from me?"

"I don't, Mandy. I can explain."

Cheryl knew this moment would come someday. It was no secret she was to marry Edward, so she had expected Mandy would ask her about him before now. She explained that she didn't love him, that it was all her parents' idea, and that she was trying her best to make sure it didn't happen.

"But we can't do this. I am only a waiter. How can I compete with the son of one of the most powerful men in the United States? Cheryl, think about this. We have to stop!"

Cheryl continued trying to explain, but her words were like water on the back of a duck. Mandy wasn't yielding. Then her efforts to argue were cut off by the ringing of Mandy's phone. The call was from Mr. Kojo's housekeeper. Mr. Kojo had fallen sick, and he wanted to see Mandy.

Chapter Twenty-Seven

The news of Mr. Kojo's illness spread like wildfire. He had congestive heart disease, which he had managed to keep in check until he received word that his daughter had been in an accident and was fighting for her life. The impact of the shock had caused him to have a heart attack.

Gloominess cloaked the staff at Gourmet DeStefano. Besides being worried about Mr. Kojo, who they all felt affection for, they knew there would be a new manager. None of them were surprised when a flyer was posted on the staff notice board two days later stating that the new general manager would be Mr. Boaz.

Mandy missed work for several days to take care of things for Mr. Kojo, who was in intensive care at the hospital. When he returned, he was asked to meet with the new manager. He got to the door and saw that the nameplate had already been changed. In bold gold letters, it now read Alex Boaz—General Manager. He knocked, and the raspy voice of Mr. Boaz answered from inside.

"Come in."

Mandy entered and bowed slightly in his usual custom. "Good morning, sir."

Mr. Boaz looked at him, nodded, and continued typing on his computer. Mandy stood there with both hands clasped in front of him, his eyes perusing the office's new decor. Mr. Boaz had changed a lot of things. He had gotten new window blinds and stocked the bar beside the window with assorted wines and liquors. The bar had been nearly empty, with just two or three bottles of wine for visitors to drink, because Mr. Kojo had been sober for the past eighteen years. The flower vase had also been changed, as had the chairs. Mr. Boaz really had good taste; Mandy had to admit. He was a relatively young man, but it seemed obvious that he had longed to take over this office for quite some time. Otherwise he wouldn't have made so many changes to the office in such a short time.

Mr. Boaz passed a ledger book over to Mandy. Mandy took it and opened it. It was the hotel's payroll.

"Your name isn't on the payroll, and you've been working here for...how long? Six, seven months?" Mr. Boaz asked.

Mandy froze. He tapped his fingers lightly on the open ledger, thinking of a way to escape this looming danger.

"Have you been working for free? I mean, has it been community service all along?" Mr. Boaz asked sarcastically.

"No," Mandy stammered.

Mr. Boaz waited for him to explain, but Mandy didn't

Shadows of Exile

have any explanation to give. "Let me guess, Mr. Kojo was paying you cash from his own money?"

"Yeah..." Mandy blurted.

"Wow! How thoughtful of him. I'm sure he only wanted to help an undocumented immigrant make a little money to survive the harsh streets of Brooklyn."

Mandy did not know if this man was taunting him or truly being compassionate. He just stood there staring at him. He did not know if he should affirm his assertion or counter it. He did not know if it would be best to lie that Mr. Kojo paid him that way because there had been no vacancy and he just wanted to help him out, or just come clean and tell him that it was because he didn't have legal papers to live or work in the United States. Maybe this was the best thing to do, he thought. After all, Mr. Boaz knew he was good at his job and the customers and guests all liked him.

"Am I wrong?" Mr. Boaz continued, "Do you have your papers?"

Mandy shook his head.

"I knew it! I knew it!" he exclaimed. "I knew there was something fishy about you. So you're undocumented, and you're flirting with Cheryl? Are you doing it for the papers?"

"No...no...I'm not," Mandy stammered. He couldn't believe his ears. He wondered how Mr. Boaz had found out about him and Cheryl. He thought only Samantha and his roommate Raheem knew he was friends with

Cheryl. Could it be that they had discussed this with other staff? "I am not flirting with her. We are just—"

"Shh. Save it. It's not really my business who you decide to flirt with or whose pants you get into to get your papers. But right now, I'll need you to provide those papers before the end of work today or I'll have to fire you."

Mandy rushed out of the building without taking off his work clothes. He feared that Mr. Boaz would not really give him the whole day to produce those papers. Maybe he only wanted him to stay in the building so the immigration officials could come and pick him up. He didn't want to go to the common room because he feared someone might tip Mr. Boaz off to the fact Mandy was about to run away. Mandy left the hotel and went straight home. He lay on his bed and cried out of desperation, wondering when all his troubles would end.

* * *

For two days, Mandy did not take Cheryl's calls. He missed spending time with her, but he willed himself to stay away from her. He would watch his phone ring again and again, but even though talking to her was the only thing that could make him feel whole again, it still seemed like a very bad idea. If someone as vindictive as Mr. Boaz had found out that he was undocumented, he wondered how many other people must have heard it by now and if any of them had been wicked enough to send his information to the authorities.

Mandy felt like he was sitting on a ticking time bomb—one that would soon explode and tear him to shreds. He felt certain that he had lost the benevolence of Mr. Kojo. He was sure that the man would not want to see him again if he returned from the hospital and heard he was hanging out with the boss' daughter. He would see him as a social climber, an opportunist who was trying to take advantage of his goodwill. Besides, he didn't know how things would turn out for Mr. Kojo when he returned from the hospital. There was a high possibility that his health would not let him return to active service, and even if he could return, there could still be trouble if Mr. Boaz told the boss that Mr. Kojo had hired an illegal immigrant and even hid him. Mandy cried bitterly. He hated himself for burning the bridges that had led him to the path of hope.

After refusing to pick up for two days, Mandy answered Cheryl's call on the third day. The phone had rung more than twelve times, and he was tired of being a coward. He decided to come right out and tell her he didn't want to see her again. He answered, and as soon he heard the sadness in her voice, he felt his armor falling off.

"Why are you avoiding me, Mandy? What have I done to deserve this?" she asked.

Mandy couldn't answer.

"I've been under a lot of pressure at home, and all I wanted was to talk to you. Even if you don't want to be with me, do you not care that I'm about to be forced into a life of unhappiness?"

The sound of her voice broke his heart into pieces. He wished he could make her his own forever. He wished he could make all her pains go away, but there was nothing he could do.

"Where are you, Mandy? I know you left your job. I've been looking for you."

"Cheryl, I am sorry. This is really hard for me, but I can't keep seeing you. I might not be here much longer."

"What are you talking about? I know you're scared of my father, but he's not going to kill you. I've told him that I'm in love with someone else, and he just has to accept it, but how can I make him accept you if you keep avoiding me? Mandy, you're hurting me so badly."

"I am sorry, babe. I am really sorry. God knows I love you. But this is more complicated than you think."

"Then open up to me! Tell me what's happening. I need to know before I go crazy."

"I'll tell you when the time is right. I promise I'll tell you. But for now, I just need some space. It's for the best. Believe me."

He ended the call and turned off his phone. Then he curled up on the bed and cried himself to sleep.

* * *

The Hugo mansion became hell for Cheryl the day her dad announced that Edward and his parents were coming over for dinner that weekend. He announced that Edward was going to pop the question on that day in the presence of both of their families.

At home, Mr. Hugo was not the jovial and kind man he appeared as to the outside world. Instead, he was a dictator who never allowed his wife or daughter to object to his rules and orders. Cheryl had told him several times that she didn't want to marry Edward, but she knew she was flogging a dead horse.

She wondered why she was so unlucky in love. All of the boyfriends she'd had in college had turned out to be no good. Now, for the first time, she was genuinely in love, and the man she loved was too scared to fight for her.

She left several voice messages, emails, and texts for Mandy, but she got no response. Most days, she cried herself to sleep, making up her mind not to dial his number again, to delete his pictures, and to block his email address, but the moment she woke, the walls of defense she had built the night before came crashing down, and she immediately picked up her phone and started to call him again.

As the day of the dinner drew closer, Cheryl became a shadow of herself. She had no shoulder to lean on. Talking to Samantha was not enough to ease her pain. She felt like she was all alone in the world, like she was nothing but a piece of merchandise about to be sold off to the highest bidder. She couldn't stand it. Thinking about what the future held for her, she made a decision—a decision she had no plans of going back on.

Chapter Twenty-Eight

Raheem tried to be the friend and brother Mandy needed. Mandy did not have enough money to buy food or pay the rent anymore, but Raheem didn't mind. He always came home with groceries and some food from the restaurant for Mandy to eat while he searched for another job.

When Mandy had started off with Cheryl, Raheem warned him to stay away from her, especially after Mandy told him he was undocumented. Raheem warned that dating her might be the end of him, but right now, as he watched Mandy turn off his phone each time Cheryl called, he felt bad to see Mandy hurting himself and the one person that truly loved him.

"Why are you doing this?" Raheem asked as Mandy rejected the call again and rolled to the other side of the bed.

"Doing what?" Mandy snapped.

"Hurting yourself. Hurting her," Raheem said. He dropped the shoe he was polishing and took a seat on the worn-out couch.

"Because I'm hanging from a cliff and I don't want to continue shaking the foundation of that cliff," Mandy replied.

"Is that why you deny yourself the only happiness you can get at the moment? Do you know you can step out of this door to go get something at the grocery store down the street, and INS could nab you and send you right back to Africa? Do you know they can knock on the door right now, and before sunset tomorrow, you'd be back in your country?"

Raheem continued trying to convince him to stop with his madness, but Mandy was adamant. He just couldn't get himself to yield to the one thing his heart desired more than anything else. Tired of arguing with him, Raheem left Mandy and went out.

A few hours later, there was a gentle knock on the door. Mandy's heart sank deep into his belly. They hadn't had a visitor as long as he had been there.

He looked through the peephole in the door and saw Cheryl standing there, wearing dark shades over her eyes. He felt the tension in his chest ease, and a smile he couldn't explain spread over his face. He opened the door and moved aside for her to come in.

"Why are you avoiding me? Don't you care about the way I feel?" she cried.

She took off the dark shades, and Mandy saw her bloodshot eyes, which were swollen from crying so much.

"I'm sorry, baby," he said. He grabbed her hands. "I didn't mean to. I'm just confused. And I have some things I need to tell you." He sat on the bed.

"How did you find this place? Did Raheem—?"

"No. I asked Samantha to find out. But what does it matter? I just came to say that I am sorry for putting you through the pain of loving me. I am moving away, and you may not see me again." She sat down beside him.

"What? You're moving where?"

"I don't know. My parents are planning an engagement dinner for me and Edward this weekend. I can't let it happen, and no one wants to hear me out, so it's better I go somewhere I can start fresh."

Mandy's heart was heavy. He touched her swollen face. "Baby, please don't go away. I don't know how I'd cope without you."

"Oh, please. Spare me the nonsense!" she snapped, and quickly stood. "You've been avoiding me, and now you want to start singing love songs? Is this a joke to you? I doubt if you ever loved me, because if you did, you wouldn't be such a coward."

Mandy closed his eyes, slapped himself twice on the forehead, and took a deep breath. It was finally time to tell her the truth.

"I'm undocumented," he blurted. "I'm scared of getting into trouble because if I get deported back to Mali, I'll be killed!"

Cheryl was dumbfounded. She lowered herself back onto the bed and listened closely as Mandy told her his story. He told her everything, from the night his uncle attacked the palace to the day he snuck into DeStefano to steal food.

He cried bitterly as he poured his heart out. Cheryl couldn't control her tears either. She held him close and patted his back as his tears soaked her black T-shirt.

"Baby, let's elope," she said.

He paused for a moment. "Elope to where?"

"Mexico, France, the Caribbean, anywhere."

Mandy thought about it for a moment and shook his head. He explained that he couldn't leave the country. If he tried to get on an international flight, the authorities would nab him and send him back to his home country.

"Then let's get married."

"What? Let's do what?" Mandy stammered.

"Let's get married. Once we're married, no one can deport you back to Africa. It's our only way out."

* * *

At nine in the morning, Mandy and Raheem were sitting in the back seat of a taxi on their way to the courthouse. Mandy was grinning from ear to ear as Raheem teased him about how good he looked in his borrowed black tuxedo. Cheryl had paid for a small apartment in Queens, where they would live after the wedding. Raheem would miss him, but he was happy his friend had finally gotten the nerve to do what he should have done a long time ago.

Cheryl had called when she left for the courthouse with Samantha. After the call, she turned off her phone so her family wouldn't be able to reach her and went to the courthouse, where she waited for her handsome groom to meet her.

Mandy's taxi was stuck in traffic just twenty minutes away when his phone rang. It was a strange number he didn't recognize. He declined the call and put it back in his pocket. The phone rang again and again.

"Your lady admirers are already calling?" Raheem teased. "I bet they'll die when they hear the heartbreaking story you're about to write."

Just then, the phone rang again. Mandy smiled and answered.

"Hello, is this Musa?" a distressed female voice asked.

Mandy was shocked to hear his old name. "What? Who is this?"

"Am I speaking with Musa?" the woman asked.

"Yes, yes. This is Musa. Who is this, and how do you know my name?"

"I am Tammy, Hamza's girlfriend," the voice said.

"Hamza? How? Hamza? Where is he?" Mandy stammered.

"Something's happened to Hamza. I've been trying for weeks to track you down. He needs a family member here quickly. Please come as soon as you can," she pleaded.

"What happened to him? Where are you?" he asked.

"I've been advised by the doctors not to discuss any details over the phone," the girl said.

"We are in D.C. I'll text you the address now."

"I'll come right away! But how did you...?" Mandy had dozens of questions, but before he could ask even one, the call ended and a text popped up with the name of a train station in Northern Virginia.

"Driver, please pull over," Mandy said.

"What? What's the matter? Who was that?" Raheem asked.

"My brother is very sick. I need to get to Washington, D.C. Driver, please pull over."

"What? A brother? Mandy, have you lost your mind? Did you forget you're getting married today? In, like, ten minutes? Let's get this done. Come on!" Raheem pleaded as the driver maneuvered through the gridlock to the curb.

"I can't. Look, go on to the courthouse and tell Cheryl that I'll explain when I get to D.C. There are a lot of things I need to tell her, but right now I have to take care of a family emergency. I'll explain everything when I can."

Mandy stepped out of the car, dashed to the other side of the street, and disappeared into the crowd. Raheem, not knowing what else to do, continued to the courthouse and found Cheryl waiting eagerly for them. She looked confused when only Raheem got out of the taxi.

"Where is he?" she asked, pacing back and forth, half hoping they were trying to play a prank on her.

"Cheryl, calm down. Let me explain. He needed to...," Raheem stammered.

As he was trying to gather his words, the blaring sound of police sirens filled the air. Two police cars swept in, and five men piled out. There were two police officers and two immigration officers. The fifth man was Mr. Boaz.

"Miss Hugo, I'm Agent Charles," one of the immigration officers said, and flashed a badge. "Can you tell me where I might find Mr. Mandy Patrick? We understand the two of you have a little something special planned at the courthouse today."

Cheryl was confused. None of this made sense to her. She couldn't understand why Mr. Boaz was with the officers. What business did he have with her affairs? Above all, she wondered how he had found out they were here to get married. She and Mandy had agreed not to tell anyone but Samantha and Raheem.

"As you can see, there's no Mandy here," Cheryl barked at them.

"So, where is he?" the officer asked.

"Why not ask your mole?" she said, looking at Mr. Boaz with a sneer.

The officers turned and looked at Mr. Boaz suspiciously, as though they were wondering if he'd misled them. Mr. Boaz, not knowing what to do, turned to Samantha and said, "But you said he'd be here. You said you were sure!"

Cheryl's mouth hung open. "Samantha! How could you?"

Samantha turned her face away.

***

Mandy sat on the train for over five hours, his mind racing. He wondered what had happened to Hamza that made his girlfriend sound so paranoid. He couldn't wait to see him, to hug him, and to tell him of all the ups and downs he had been through since he'd arrived in the U.S. He wondered if Hamza was mad at him. Was that why he never responded to any of Mandy's emails? He knew they had a lot to talk about, but first Mandy needed to know what was wrong with him and find a way to help him.

When they were about twenty minutes away from Union Station, Mandy called Tammy, but she didn't answer the phone. He tried a few more times, but it just rang with no answer. He then sent a text to let her know his estimated arrival time.

The train stopped at Union Station, and the travelers disembarked. The train station was crowded with people boarding and exiting the train. Mandy stood on the platform, pulled out his phone, and dialed Tammy's number one more time. After seven rings, which seemed to last for eternity, she finally picked up.

"Hello. I am at the station. Where are you?"

"We're by the waiting area near the train gates. What are you wearing?" she asked.

"A black tuxedo with a white shirt and red tie," he said, looking around. He saw a blond lady standing close to a pillar waving at him. "Is that you in the blue dress?"

he asked, but before she could answer, he saw his brother Hamza standing next to her. "Hamza!" he screamed, running toward them. He gave Hamza a big hug and held him tight.

Hamza stood transfixed, with a look of confusion all over his face.

"Hamza, I missed you so much. How have you been?" Mandy asked, tears rolling down his cheeks. "I'm so glad you're okay. I thought something had happened to you," Mandy continued as he gave Hamza another hug, squeezing him even tighter this time. He then leaned back, looking into Hamza's familiar eyes.

"Musa? Where's Mom and Dad? Where is Menkiti?"

Mandy's jaw dropped. He stared at Tammy for a brief second in confusion, and then he turned back to Hamza. Flashes of images of the massacre at the palace, his parents' lifeless bodies, and Menkiti went through his mind. The noise of the trains and crowds suddenly faded. He could see Tammy's lips moving, but he couldn't hear a word she was saying.

The entire station was spinning. Everything went pitch black.

The journey continues...

Acknowledgments

To all the countless strangers who opened up their hearts and homes to an immigrant kid from Africa. You were my shelter during the storms, and warmth during the blistering winters. My journey would not have been possible without you, and for that I am forever grateful.

Made in the USA
Middletown, DE
08 January 2020

82822767R00177